BOUND TO BIL

Doms of Destiny, Colorado 2

Chloe Lang

MENAGE EVERLASTING

Siren Publishing, Inc.
www.SirenPublishing.com

A SIREN PUBLISHING BOOK
IMPRINT: Ménage Everlasting

BOUND TO BILLIONAIRES
Copyright © 2013 by Chloe Lang

ISBN: 978-1-62740-150-0

First Printing: June 2013

Cover design by Les Byerley
All art and logo copyright © 2013 by Siren Publishing, Inc.

Printed in the U.S.A.

PUBLISHER
Siren Publishing, Inc.
www.SirenPublishing.com

DEDICATION

Without Chloe Vale I wouldn't be able to do what I do. She's a friend and a supporter. She works hard on my books and they wouldn't be the same without her. I love having her as a partner in my career.

With all my heart, I thank you, Chloe. This book is dedicated to you.

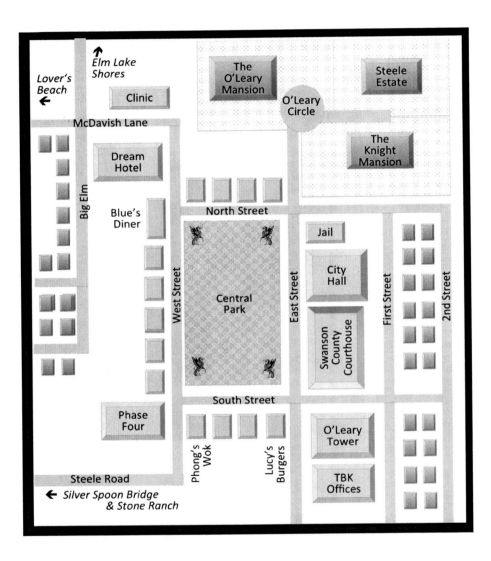

BOUND TO BILLIONAIRES

Doms of Destiny, Colorado 2

CHLOE LANG
Copyright © 2013

Prologue

Sitting on the sofa, Megan Lunceford looked at the man being handcuffed by the FBI agents.

"Mrs. Lunceford, when did you first meet your husband?" The agent's voice seemed far away and faint.

She was still getting used to being called "Mrs. Lunceford." Kip had said he was thrilled when she agreed to take his name instead of keeping her maiden name. In truth, "Lunceford" was a slight improvement, if only slight, for her. She'd been so happy to say good-bye to "Ramsbottom," which had been used against her by cruel classmates from elementary all the way up to high school. Right now, she would've loved to have it back.

"I met Kip thirty days ago," she answered, hearing the flatness in her tone. "April first to be exact."

The day of fools.

Appropriate. Really appropriate.

Kip's eyes were wide, but he wore the same twisted grin on his face as the one on the day she'd married him.

"You were married in Vegas this past Saturday, correct?"

She nodded. Her entire body felt like lead. The agents had come into her home, the house her mother had left her. She needed her mother right now. Her mom would know what to do.

"How old are you, Mrs. Lunceford?"

"I turned twenty on February fourth, three months ago." It had to have been the worst birthday in the history of mankind.

The image of her mother in the hospital bed, taking her last breath, floated to the front of her mind. Alone, she'd held her mom's hand. Like her, her mother was an only child. No siblings. No husband. No one. They'd only had each other. Her mom had died just three months ago, and two months later, she'd met Kip, though it felt more like multiple eternities.

"Mrs. Lunceford?"

What would you think about your little girl now, Mom? I've really screwed up.

"Mrs. Lunceford?"

Kip had come to her at the lowest point in her life. Guys never noticed her, but he did. Her dull, grief-stricken days had been softened by his charisma. She'd fallen for his charm. What an idiot she'd been. Was he some kind of homicidal psycho?

"Mrs. Lunceford?"

Her head spun like a Texas tornado complete with every kind of mental debris imaginable. What did she really know about her husband? He claimed to be a software developer, but was that even true? Was anything he'd said to her true? Before tying the knot, he'd filled her ears with hundreds of compliments. Were they all lies, too? They must've been.

She looked down at her breasts and hips, which were too big for her frame. On their honeymoon, Kip had shown another side of himself to her—a side that didn't see her as beautiful. His other side, the charming Kip, was a goddamn liar.

"Are you okay, Mrs. Lunceford? Do you need a glass of water?"

The insanity of what was going on around her, the gloved strangers rifling through her things—her mother's things—filled her with panic. She watched Kip be led out the door by two agents.

Where were they taking him? Away. That was one good thing about this entire mess.

With her husband gone, she turned her attention to the commotion in the house. The lawmen were loading up boxes and boxes with her belongings. Nothing was safe from them. Even the furniture was being removed to the front lawn. What would her mother's longtime neighbors be thinking about all this?

"Are your men going to take everything I own, Agent Crow?" She looked the man directly in the eyes.

He didn't answer.

A female agent, wearing navy slacks and blazer, walked through the door and took a seat in the chair opposite Megan. Her straight, dark hair was cut short at chin length. "Agent Crow, I've got this. Thank you."

He nodded and headed to the kitchen where Megan could hear pots and pans being pulled out of the cabinets.

"The rest of you." The woman's voice was raised. "Give me the room."

The men emptied into the other parts of the house. Megan's trepidation muted ever so slightly. It was the first sliver of quiet she'd had since the front door had been busted open by the FBI. She thought about thanking the woman for the gesture but didn't. The female agent looked grim and serious, so Megan kept her mouth shut.

"Let me introduce myself, Mrs. Lunceford." Unsmiling, the woman held out her hand. Megan shook it. "I'm Special Agent Brown. I'm the field lead on this case."

"Do I need an attorney, Agent?" She looked Brown directly in the eyes, fearing what her answer would be.

"Yes, but there's plenty of time for you to call your lawyer after we take you downtown." Brown took out a notepad and wrote something on its pages. "I'll have Agent Crow take you, Mrs. Lunceford."

"Give me the address. I can drive myself."

The agent shook her head. "The cars are being seized by my men, too."

Why were they taking her vehicle? "My car isn't worth anything to anyone but me, Agent. It's a 1978 model. Kip's is new."

"I saw the brand-new Maserati in your driveway. It doesn't fit this neighborhood, does it?"

Megan ignored the thinly veiled sarcasm in Brown's timbre. She must save Granny Gremlin. Her mother had given her the car when she'd turned sixteen. That had been a great birthday. "Please, Agent Brown. Whatever Kip was involved in, I wasn't. You've got to believe me."

"We'll sort all this out, Mrs. Lunceford. I think it would be best to get you out of here." The woman stood. "Surely, you don't want to see my guys strip your house clean."

Defeated, she answered in a soft breath. "I don't. What is my husband being arrested for?" By the way the FBI was operating, innocent-until-proven-guilty didn't seem to apply here.

"Espionage and conspiracy against the United States government."

Her heart skipped several beats. *A spy? I married a spy?* "Where are you taking him?"

"I can't tell you that right now since he's been classified at the highest threat level against the United States."

"When can you tell me?" she asked.

"I don't know the answer to that now, but I'm sure as soon as it's determined to be safe, you'll be told where he is." Brown looked at her in a way that screamed pity. "Are you ready to go, Mrs. Lunceford?"

"I guess so." *God, how had this all happened?*

* * * *

Eric Knight walked out of the FBI's interrogation room with his brother, Scott.

"I can't believe that it's finally over," Scott said as they walked to the bank of elevators. "We almost lost everything."

"We're not out of the woods yet." He placed his Stetson on his head, trying to reclaim a sense of normalcy. It didn't come. "Homeland Security is still going through all our files." His hands balled up into fists. Kip Lunceford had betrayed them.

"Bro, we're innocent of this. This is all on Kip. We've cooperated in every way the government has asked us to. Our company is fine."

"Fine? We'll be lucky if we can turn this debacle around."

Scott pushed the button to call the elevator. "We've been cleared. We should celebrate."

"Celebrate the fact that one of our most trusted employees duped us." Guilt and rage twisted his gut into knots. "We may not have been the traitors, Scott, but we're not innocent in this. We should've seen Lunceford for who he is."

"There's no blood on our hands. None."

"You don't buy that any more than I do. Our code will be used against our brothers on the battlefield, Scott. Our code. Every medal we earned in Afghanistan should be returned."

Scott's face darkened. "Let it go, Eric. It will eat you alive if you don't."

"Take your own advice, brother. You're as tore up about this fucking disaster as I am."

"True. It will take time but we will turn the company and ourselves around. Trust me."

"You're the only one I'll ever trust again, Scott."

"Same here."

The elevator doors opened and Eric stepped inside. "I swear if he had any accomplices, Scott, I'll crush them with my bare hands."

Chapter One

Five years later

Lofty, snow-covered peaks, tall pines, and incredible wildlife had been in view for over an hour since Megan Lunceford had left Highway 230 and turned onto Holyroyd Road. Even though the natural beauty was quite stunning, she couldn't truly appreciate the surroundings just outside Granny Gremlin's windshield.

She glanced at herself in the rearview mirror and frowned before sending her attention back to the road. Her hair was disheveled and her makeup was in major need of a touch-up. But even with the best cosmetics money could buy, which she definitely didn't have, the twinkle in her eye her mother had so loved was missing. It had been gone for a very long time. She looked more like a refugee than a woman about to appear in court.

Like a ghost from the past, she recalled her husband's silky words on their wedding night. "You're a porcelain doll, babe. Too pretty for words."

Unfortunately the lying bastard never tired of words. Why had she been such an idiot? She would've never been swept off her feet by Kip if her mother had lived. Two months after her funeral and fifteen pounds heavier, she'd bumped into the Asshole at the coffee shop down the block from her mom's place. His toothy grin and sugary-sweet compliments had come out of the blue when her grief had drained away her reserves of logic and will. The chance to fill her days and nights with something other than her loneliness had sealed the deal. Now, she prayed for a magic wand that could transport her back to that day he'd knelt in front of her and proposed. Instead of saying "yes" with tears streaming down her cheeks, she would kick him in the balls and run for the door. Too bad the world had no magic or miracles. She could really use some right now.

Her digits gripped the steering wheel like ten tiny vises and her left foot hovered over the brake like a police helicopter. She wasn't used to driving in the mountains, and though a normal driver would likely only use the brake going downhill, she'd kept her left foot there the entire way to calm her nerves. Since turning onto this lane, the drive had been uphill nearly the whole way. Now, it was a steep downhill trek. Even at the current fifteen-miles-per-hour pace, her ears continued to pop from the change in pressure due to the elevation. She had been ordered to appear in court in Destiny today. The way to the small town in Northern Colorado was rough, twisty, and terrifying with its narrow passages and steep drop-offs.

To get to the turnoff to Destiny, she'd actually had to drive out of Colorado and into Wyoming a few miles, since the only road to the town was there. It had only taken her a little over three hours to cover the one hundred and sixty-six miles from Denver to the turn, but the past eighteen miles had taken her over an hour. As she came over the last ridge, the grade of the road softened, dipping down into a valley with the most beautiful mountain lake she'd ever seen. On a peninsula that nearly divided Elm Lake in half was the place she'd been journeying to for seventeen hours straight. As gorgeous as the space was, her heart sank from loneliness. Her mother's house in Dallas was a very long way from Destiny.

She glanced at the folders in the passenger seat next to her and then once again to the road that, according to her map, wrapped around the large lake. Her whole financial life had been distilled into the pages inside those folders. The verdict? Flat broke. Destitute. Cleaned out.

Cash? The fifteen dollars and change in her purse was the extent of her personal fortune.

What were the attorneys at Two Black Knights Enterprises thinking?

Her husband, hopefully soon-to-be ex-husband, had been a longtime employee at TBK. They should be going after him, not her, though getting through the government's red tape had proven impossible.

The special agent had been wrong that she would be told Kip's whereabouts. Was Brown just trying to appease her during his arrest? Probably.

After all these years, Kip's classification had never changed from the highest threat level. To the United States government, he was a terrorist. Clearly they weren't interested in telling her a damn thing. So she'd been unable to keep track of Kip in the system.

Sure, she'd gotten his letters filled with crazy ramblings and serious threats, but none of them had any return addresses on them to help her locate his prison. Even with the postmarks indicating the cities of origin on every envelope, they only led to dead ends. None of the towns had prisons.

She came up to the blinking red light strung from two poles on opposite corners of the intersection. There wasn't another vehicle in sight, so she found it odd to see a traffic signal out here in the middle of nowhere. On one of the corners of the intersection was a large, elk-shaped wooden sign. Painted on it were three arrows, each with directions. The arrow pointing ahead read "The Double L Ranch." The sign that led drivers right had the words "Stone Ranch."

But where she needed to go was left.

Its arrow had an ominous word that filled her with anxiety. "Destiny." Seven letters. Most might find the word to be hopeful. Not her. Not after everything that had happened.

Fate had been ugly to Megan. More than ugly. Before marrying Kip, she believed in possibilities, much like her mother had before she'd died. No more. She flipped on her blinker out of habit more than anything and turned on the road to Destiny. Life had been cruel, but she knew it could turn even darker.

Coming to the bridge that crossed a wash, she peered at the sign that marked the limits of the town's border. "Welcome to Destiny, the best-kept secret in Colorado."

The first building she drove by was three stories tall with two balconies. The arched windows on the two upper floors, with their wide, white molding, were impressive. The name of the building on the sign that hung from the lower balcony puzzled her. What could Phase Four be?

It didn't matter.

She was due in the Swanson County Courthouse. It was on East Street. She looked at the time on her cell.

Eleven twenty-nine. Her hearing was set for eleven thirty. One minute later and she would be in contempt of court.

Her heart sank.

She turned right onto South Street and saw the park in the center of the city's square on her left.

The dragon statues on the square's corners looked out of place but impressive. The courthouse, now within her view, appeared terrifying and ominous. Like most buildings of its ilk, it was made of stone. A statue of a man holding up a torch, much like the Statue of Liberty, stood before the entrance. Where was Justice with its blindfold and scales? Did the Destiny judicial system have its own way of doing things? She hoped so. Her past dealings with other entities of the law like the FBI and Homeland Security had been less about right and wrong and more about screwing her over and keeping her in the dark.

Turning left on East Street, she parked her car in one of the spots in front of the courthouse. After she removed the key from the ignition, Granny Gremlin sputtered and coughed for a couple of seconds before finally turning off.

Taking a deep breath, she turned the rearview mirror so she could get a better look at herself. No time for a redo. After a quick couple of strokes of the brush through her hair, she got out of the car. Across the park, she could see the local inn—the Dream Hotel. It reminded her of a gingerbread house more than anything else. God, how she wished her credit cards still worked. A bath and a bed would be heaven right now. Not happening. Her motel for tonight would be the rest area she'd passed near the Wyoming-Colorado border. Her bed? Granny Gremlin.

She grabbed the files and headed up the steps past the doomful marble columns. What difference did this hearing make now? Except for her mother's home and Granny Gremlin, she didn't have anything. Everything else was gone—even her mother's diary.

* * * *

Eric Knight leaned against the mahogany half wall dividing the courtroom in two. He wasn't surprised to see so many friends and neighbors in the public gallery. One thing about his hometown, everyone flocked to each other's sides to help...and to gawk, especially when there was a possible scandal.

"Looks like all of Destiny is here this afternoon," Scott said.

Like Eric, his brother's cowboy clothes were gone, replaced by a dark gray suit and red tie. The only sign that ranching was in his brother's DNA were the boots sticking out from the bottom of his pants. Damn. Eric wished he'd thought of that. Instead, he was wearing loafers. At least they were leather and black, appropriate Dom material and color.

Nodding, he looked over at Scott. "Quite the turnout."

"Look over there." His brother pointed to the Stone brothers and Amber, their new woman. "The playboys of Destiny have been tamed."

Eric feigned a mocking frown and hit Scott in the upper arm. "What the fuck do you mean by that? We're the reigning playboys. Always have been. Not the Stones."

He watched Emmett, the eldest of the three, smile and wave.

"Shit." Eric waved back. He lowered his voice. "It's been so long since I've been in here I forgot how good the acoustics are."

"Best to use that to our advantage then, bro." Scott upped his volume. "I'm thinking we go to Phase Four tonight, Eric." His brother winked and looked at every unattached woman in the room. "We might need company. What do you think?"

"I think your cock's happiness is all you care about."

"Come on, Eric. You don't care about yours? I know better and so do a few of the women in here."

"Sit down, guys." Cameron Strange adjusted his tie.

As their attorney, he'd advised them to wear the corporate drag to court. Eric and Scott had resisted but knew Cameron was right. The Swanson County judge, Ethel O'Leary, was a sweetheart, but when it came to the law and her court, she was a stickler and unbending. Eric remembered the first time he'd been in here with Ethel behind the big desk, high above the rest of the crowd. He and Scott and the other orphan boys had gotten into some mischief. Ethel had handled them all with a heavy hand. Thank God for her.

Behind them sat Dylan, Cameron's brother. He wore his characteristic dark suit. Dylan's shades were tucked away, since they were in a courtroom, but Eric knew they would be on his face the moment he stepped out of here. Courtrooms and churches were the only places he'd ever seen Dylan remove his shades, which were part of the man's signature look. Dylan was a trusted friend long before being hired to lead TBK's security arm. He'd singlehandedly discovered the origin of the hack—Megan Lunceford's home.

Dylan leaned over the gallery wall. "That's her." He pointed to the doors at the back of the courtroom. "That's Kip's wife."

She looked like a little princess to Eric, not like a fire-breathing dragon about to storm the castle like he'd imagined. How could Kip have landed such a beautiful woman? She bumped into Mitchell Wolfe, the sheriff's trouble-seeking brother, who was holding a folder. The collision caused his papers to fly in every direction.

"I'm so sorry," she said in the sweetest tone he'd ever heard.

"Wow," Scott said, mirroring his sentiments exactly.

Eric stared as Mrs. Lunceford bent down to help Mitchell collect his things. Her white blouse bulged with ample, magnificent breasts. God, what Dom wouldn't want to cup those mounds in his hands, pinch their twin nipples, and enjoy the sweet moans from those gorgeous lips?

She wore a skirt, which he liked on women much better than slacks. Her shapely legs made Eric's cock stir. That bastard Kip may have screwed Scott and him, but he couldn't help but admire the man's taste in women. She was curvy in all the right places. God, he would love getting a taste of her delights. Lunceford's wife was a mouthwatering morsel by any standards, especially his.

"Damn, who knew?" Scott said beside him.

"Again, I'm so sorry," Megan said to Wolfe as she handed him his stack of papers.

"Don't give it a thought, miss." Mitchell's sudden interest in her didn't sit well with Eric. Why? He wasn't sure, but it definitely didn't. "My brother is sheriff here, and today he's acting as an officer of the court." Mitchell pointed to Jason, who was in his uniform with his holstered gun standing next to his deputy, Charlie Blake. Both men were by the door to the judge's chambers. "His job is to protect the courtroom during the trial."

She smiled at Mitchell before turning and walking up the center aisle. Her shoes tapped against the wooden floor, making Eric's pulse grow hot with every sweet sway of her hips. She'd fucked TBK over. He'd enjoy fucking her until she couldn't see straight, much less walk. Not one to take a second look at another man's wife, he scanned her like an MRI. Kip wasn't a real man. He was a traitor, not just to TBK or him and Scott, but also to the United States of America.

Scott leaned in as she took a seat at the table to the side of them facing forward. "Can you imagine how sweet that little vixen would look chained up in our dungeon?"

Yes, he could. In fact, Eric was imagining it right now. Not a good thing to let his mind wander to such ideas. He needed to stay focused.

Dylan was certain about his findings. The new project he and Scott were developing for the Pentagon had been attacked several times by a malicious code from Megan's computer.

She's the enemy. Keep your dick in your pants and out of this hearing.

Easy to say to himself, but much harder to do. Seeing her delicate fingers tremble as she arranged her folders in front of her, it was next to impossible. This wasn't the way he'd seen the day going.

As the judge entered from her chambers, the bailiff spoke. "All rise. The Swanson County Court for the District of Northern Colorado is in session, the Honorable Judge Ethel O'Leary presiding. All having business before this court draw near, give attention, and you shall be heard. You may be seated."

Ethel was in her black robe, which accentuated her silver locks beautifully. Hard to believe she had turned seventy-nine last March. She was the wife of Patrick and Sam O'Leary, descendants of the founders of Destiny, and next-door neighbors of Scott and him.

Ethel pounded her gavel. "This court is now in session. I have before me the case of TBK versus Megan Lunceford. Are all parties and their attorneys present?" She gazed at Kip's wife.

"Yes, Your Honor," Cameron said on Eric and Scott's behalf. "Two Black Knights Enterprises are here."

Ethel turned her stare to their table. "And TBK's copresidents, too. Eric, you look good in a suit."

"Thank you, ma'am."

Ethel smiled at Eric like a proud parent before turning to his brother. "Scott, you look uncomfortable to me."

"You're right about that," his brother answered.

"Do you all know each other?" Megan asked meekly.

"Destiny is a small town, miss." Ethel leaned forward. "Trust me, young lady, this court will be impartial and fair. Mr. Strange, you are acting legal counsel for the plaintiffs, correct?"

"Yes, Judge," Cam answered.

The judge's eyes narrowed. "Just one attorney? I would think a billion-dollar company like Two Black Knights would have a sea of lawyers at their disposal. Why just one?"

Cam bristled. "I assure the court that we are more than prepared to present our case."

Ethel waved him off and turned to the beautiful defendant. "And I assume you are…" She looked down at a paper in front of her. "…Megan Lunceford. Is that correct?" The judge looked back at her.

She blinked. "Yes, Your Honor."

Ethel leaned forward slightly. "Are you an attorney, Mrs. Lunceford?"

Megan shook her head. "No, ma'am."

A murmur went through the crowd. What was going on here? Was Megan going to represent herself in court?

Ethel frowned. "What is your profession?"

"I was a secretary for three years."

"Was?" Ethel asked. "And now?"

"I'm currently looking for work, Your Honor." Megan lowered her eyes as if embarrassed by the admission.

The more the little vixen talked, the more he wanted to get closer to her. But she was the enemy, right? She was the one mucking up the code, right?

Eric turned to Cam and Scott, his voice low. "Secretary, my ass. She's got to have hacking skills that would make Google, Yahoo, and all the rest weep."

"Or she's in touch with Kip, which would be my guess," his brother offered. "Look at her, guys. She doesn't look like a criminal mastermind to me."

She didn't look that way to him either. In fact, she looked more subbie than anything else, which made his lust boil hot in his veins.

"Either way," Cam said. "She's going to pay."

Ethel put on some glasses and read the papers in front of her.

Eric had never seen her wear them outside the courtroom. It made the grand lady judge look even more stately, if that was even possible.

"That's our sweetheart," Patrick whispered from a couple of rows behind.

"Ours indeed," Sam, his brother, answered. The O'Leary brothers were both in their mid-eighties. Patrick and Sam were highly decorated vets. They'd both served in the Korean War, and between them they'd earned three Purple Hearts and two Congressional Medals of Honor, among other notable accolades.

"Order in the court." Ethel pounded her gavel twice. "I will clear the courtroom if those in the gallery continue talking."

She sent a harsh stare past Eric to where her husbands sat, but then followed it up with a cute little nod. Those three were so in love even after decades of being together. They were the A-list family in Destiny. Patrick, a retired physician, earned his first million in the mid-sixties in the import business. He and Sam, the current town shrink, pooled their resources in '72 and built O'Leary Global. The two old corporate giants still ran the company and had been early advisors, though not investors, in TBK. Their knowledge had helped rocket the venture into the stratosphere. Eric and Scott had a long way to go to catch up with Patrick and Sam, whose company was currently valued at twenty-seven billion. TBK had only entered the billion-dollar club seven months ago, but if the new venture panned out, it would triple its profits in less than eighteen months, increasing the company's worth by leaps and bounds.

Ethel's voice brought him back to the present. "Mrs. Lunceford, have you brought the documents this court ordered for this hearing?"

"I have, Your Honor." Megan stood, scooping up the folders into a single pile. "Whom do I give them to?"

"The bailiff will take them, young lady." Ethel's tone was softer than Eric had ever heard it when she was wearing the black robe, more like when she was serving pancakes to the morning crowd during Dragon Week. Not good. She was taking a shine to Megan Lunceford. That wasn't good for TBK or for him.

Megan stood and handed the files to the bailiff, who then handed them to the judge.

"Miss, have you at least consulted an attorney for this case?"

The beauty turned to him. Eric got a clear view of her green eyes. The golden flecks made her look like some kind of gentle angelic creature. He could look at those eyes until the end of time.

She blinked and turned her attention back to the judge. "No, Your Honor."

Ethel rifled through several of the papers. "And the reason appears to be a lack of funds according to these records you've brought, am I right?"

"Yes, ma'am."

"When a person represents themselves in court without the assistance of an attorney, whether as the defendant or the plaintiff, and whether or not the issue before the court is criminal or civil, she is operating *pro se*, which in Latin means 'for oneself.' This right for a member of the public to represent himself, or in this case herself, predates even the US Constitution. In Colorado, as in all fifty states, it is generally considered a protected right. Did you know that?"

"No, Your Honor." Her feminine timbre was like gasoline on Eric's already-too-hot lust, searing his insides. Was this an act of hers, a way for her to get what she wanted?

"Mrs. Lunceford, most legal professionals consider a person going to court without the aid of an attorney to be a really bad idea. I agree with that assessment." Ethel looked at Cam and then back at another paper on her desk. "Ten million dollars is what TBK is seeking from this woman, correct?"

"Yes, Your Honor." Cam stood. "We will prove—"

Ethel held up her hand. "Hold your horses, Mr. Strange. This is my courtroom, not yours."

Cam nodded. "Yes, Your Honor."

"Mrs. Lunceford, have you had a chance to read the docket?"

"Yes." Megan looked nervous.

"Did you know that they are seeking this kind of settlement from you?" the judge asked.

She nodded. "But as you can see, I don't have any money."

"That's true, but should they prevail in this case, it won't be just your bank account they empty." Ethel grabbed a piece of paper. "This house in Dallas will be seized and sold to apply to damages."

"Not my mother's house." Megan's hands went up to her mouth.

Ethel scanned the papers in front of her. "It says here you inherited the house after your mother's death. Is that right?"

Tears pooled in Megan's eyes. "That's all I have, Your Honor. After the FBI and Homeland Security came after my husband, they took—"

"Objection," Cam barked.

"Sustained. Mrs. Lunceford, we'll be hearing your testimony about the events later." Ethel tapped the desktop with her fingers.

Even though Cam had kept Megan from continuing the tale of events about Kip's arrest and eventual conviction, Eric knew them like the back of his hand. He and Scott had hired Lunceford early on as their first batch of employees. Five total. Vicky, Felix, Norman, Lucy, and Kip. TBK had been tight and agile. They'd landed several consulting contracts in those first few years, and the employee roster had grown to what it was today, six hundred and thirty-three. Of the first five, only Vicky Bates and Felix Averson remained, and they had both been flown in from TBK's main offices in Dallas for today as witnesses for their side. Tonight, the two would be flying back.

Eric turned his head and saw them sitting together in the back row. Felix's hair had thinned and his gut had expanded over the years. He wore a crumpled gray suit with a navy tie. Vicky was dressed in a sharp business suit. Her makeup was impeccable and her hair was fixed perfectly—like always. Vicky was a classy lady. They were his and Scott's right and left hand, with Vicky in the role of Executive

Vice President and Felix in the role of Assistant Vice President. Lucy and Norman had married and left to follow their dream of opening up a gourmet burger joint. Lucy's Burgers was still the best place to get a hamburger in Destiny.

Kip Lunceford? The bastard's coding skills were nearly as good as his and Scott's, and in some cases better. He'd been the shining star of the original five. When TBK had been awarded the Pentagon's consulting contract to develop missile-targeting software, he and Scott had put Kip in the driver's seat of that project. Bad idea.

Eric stared at Megan, the wife of the man that nearly brought down the entire company. She wasn't the only one who the feds had decimated after discovering Kip had sold classified code to terrorists. If Patrick and Sam hadn't called in favors from some powerful senators and congressmen, they might've lost everything, too. Eric and his brother had been blindsided by the whole Kip thing. Trust wasn't a luxury they would ever give in to again. Never. Not when it came to TBK, or anything else for that matter.

"Kip's wife can't get away with this, Cam," Eric said through clenched teeth. "Ethel seems to have a soft spot when it comes to her."

"I can't blame her, bro," Scott whispered back. "She looks innocent to me, too. And if truth be known, I've got something hard between my legs for her right now."

"Don't fuck up, Scott. This is TBK's future that's on the line," Eric said. "We either stop her from hacking into our private servers and screwing up our code or we might as well throw in the towel and watch all our work be crushed into dust."

Scott's eyes never left Megan. "I hear you."

Scott's hushed tone didn't make Eric's worry fade. "I know she's beautiful, our type for sure, but that doesn't change the fact that her computer is what Dylan identified as the source, remember?"

Scott nodded. "God, she is our type, bro. Sharing her would be amazing. Can you imagine us showing up at Phase Four with her between us?"

"Not happening." Of course, that image had been in Eric's head from the moment Megan Lunceford had entered the courtroom. "Keep your head in the game or I will knock it off your shoulders."

Ethel stopped tapping and stared at Megan. "Mrs. Lunceford, would you have an attorney with you today if you had had the funds to hire one?"

Megan nodded. "Absolutely."

"Good to know." Ethel sat back in her chair. "This court will assign you an attorney to review your case."

"But, Your Honor?" Cam's frustration was evident in every syllable.

Ethel's face was stern. "No buts, Mr. Strange. Mrs. Lunceford, do you accept the offer of this court for an attorney to be assigned to you?"

"Thank you, Your Honor. I do accept." She wiped a tear from her eye. "Absolutely, I accept. I must keep my mother's home. She left it to me."

Ethel looked back down to the papers on her desk. "Back taxes. Lots of back taxes. You're in quite a fix, young lady."

"Your Honor, Mrs. Lunceford brought the papers, but what about the computer that she was ordered to bring?" Cameron asked. God, Cam was one hell of an attorney. "Where is that?"

The stately woman held up her hand to silence him. "He's right, Mrs. Lunceford. You are supposed to have a computer here with you today."

That computer was the key to everything. They had to have it.

Megan nodded. "Your Honor, I brought it, but it is quite heavy. I'm not sure why you need it. I got the computer, a monitor, and a modem from a pawn shop less than a year ago to help me look for work. A complete waste of money since the thing only turned on a couple of times. The computer is in my car out front. If I could get some help, I'll bring it in."

"Objection," Cam snapped.

"Sustained. Mrs. Lunceford, please keep your answers short or Mr. Strange might bust a blood vessel."

There were several chuckles from the gallery.

"Phoebe Blue, come up here." Ethel waved her forward. Phoebe and her brothers Corey and Shane were local. Phoebe was an attorney, Corey was a US Marshal, and Shane was…well, that was a long, sad story.

Phoebe was all business. She'd worked her way through law school on her own. Her hair, which was quite long but rarely down, was up in a bun. She walked to the judge's bench. "Yes, Your Honor."

"Counselor, let me introduce you to your newest client, Megan Lunceford."

"I'd be happy to help, ma'am, but my caseload is full." Phoebe was a friend of theirs. She clearly didn't want to be on a case that opposed TBK.

"It just got even fuller, counselor. Bailiff, please give these to Mrs. Lunceford's attorney." Ethel handed back all the papers Megan had brought to the court. "You may submit them to the court as exhibits when we come back to hear opening arguments next Tuesday at 9:00 a.m."

The bailiff took the files and gave them to Phoebe. Megan's eyes were wide as saucers in apparent shock.

"Court is adjourned." Ethel pounded her gavel on the wood.

"All rise," the bailiff said.

As Eric stood, he looked over again at Megan and had the oddest feeling wash over him. Call it a premonition, an impression, or just a silly hunch, but something about her reached into him, and he knew everything in his life was about to be changed by her. How or what? He wasn't sure, but as the court cleared, he felt it into the very core of his being.

Chapter Two

Scott Knight heard a distant crash of thunder outside the courtroom. The last thing Destiny needed was another downpour after the most recent one. There were still so many roads washed out in the area that digging out would continue for a few more weeks. But the gray day outside wasn't what was really at the front of his mind. The blonde beauty he and his brother were trying to bring down was at the top of his thoughts. Megan Lunceford.

Megan and Phoebe walked to the far corner of the courtroom.

Vicky and Felix came up from the back of the gallery together.

Felix nodded and Vicky asked in a hushed tone, "Another week? I guess this trip was a waste? How are you doing, guys?"

"We're good," Eric whispered.

Felix placed his hands on Scott's and Eric's shoulders. "We've got you covered."

"Thanks, man," Scott said softly. Felix might've aged over the years, but he still seemed like the charming guy from those first days at TBK. "You two head to Dallas. I know your plates are full with all the new contracts."

"Okay. You need us here next week?" Vicky asked.

"We'll let you know," replied Eric.

"We're going to grab a bite before we leave for Texas," Felix said. "How about joining us?"

"No thanks." Scott shook his head. "I need to talk to Eric about something."

Felix shrugged. "Next time then."

Vicky and Felix said their good-byes and left.

After they were out of earshot, Scott turned to Eric. "Kip's wife can't be involved. She doesn't look like a criminal mastermind to me."

Megan was shaking like a leaf next to Phoebe, her new court-appointed attorney.

Eric glared at him, his voice rising slightly. "Don't."

"Listen to your brother, Scott." Cameron thrummed his fingers on the plaintiff's desk. "Dylan has the goods on her. She's as guilty as they come."

She didn't look felonious to him. She looked more like an angel than a cyber thief and dubious hacker.

"I thought we were going to have this done today," Eric said to Cam.

"Ethel's added week doesn't change a thing. Mrs. Lunceford is over a barrel no matter what Phoebe tries." Cam continued looking over his files. He was a great attorney. Phoebe was just as great. They'd squared off many times in this very court, with Phoebe edging past Cam in the win column.

"And what does that get us?" Scott was no longer on board with the plan. Destroying Megan's life didn't feel right. Not now. "Eric, you always say I have a sixth sense about things. Intuition. Well, trust me. She's innocent."

Eric shifted from foot to foot, clearly agitated by Scott's words. "You think I say it as a compliment? You know better. I trust the facts, bro, and the facts are right here." He reached over and patted the pages on the table in front of Cam. "Dylan proved the insidious code came from Mrs. Lunceford's home. It's cut and dry. Capisce?"

"Give me a break." Scott wasn't about to back down. There was something about Megan that would never add up to her being behind their troubles. "You know there are ways around that. Someone could've hacked her computer."

Dylan leaned across the half wall that divided the front of the courtroom from the gallery, which was emptying quickly of Destiny residents. "You saying I don't know what I'm doing, Scott?" The investigator's tone was harsh.

"I'm saying there are all kinds of ways to frame someone in our industry. Kip proved that." He turned back to Megan's direction. She and Phoebe were heading out the side door together. "Until we're certain, I'm saying let's slow this train down. Kip has lots of contacts on the outside, including the Chinese. Just because the creep is in prison doesn't mean he can't be working with them again."

Dylan slapped him on the back. "She's gorgeous. That's a fact. But Kip isn't in a position to work with anyone. He's a traitor, not just to TBK but also to the United States. Homeland Security isn't going to let him see the light of day ever."

"If that's true—"

"It's true," Dylan reiterated.

"Fine. So how can she be working with Kip then? Isn't that what we've been thinking since we found the first virus?" The fact was that TBK's viability hinged on the new platform. The first malicious program wasn't the last. There'd been sixteen others in the past five months.

As the side door closed after Megan and Phoebe exited, Eric grabbed him by the shoulder. "Maybe what's fueling her is misplaced revenge. Her husband was taken away while he was working for us."

"Exactly my point. You remember Kip's taste in women, right?"

"God, you're not going to drop this, are you?" Eric was a hard nut to crack. "Let's don't go there for now. We've got an entire week to deal with this until our court date. What do you say, Scott?"

He shrugged. "I'm going to talk to her."

"Hell no," Cam barked. "That could put our whole case in jeopardy."

Eric took a deep breath. "Leave it alone, bro."

Scott knew he should, but he couldn't. "Listen to me. Something isn't right about this. I feel it in my bones."

"Feelings are your strong suit, not mine."

Scott nodded. "Before you close off that logical mind of yours, Eric, just listen. Okay?"

After a long sigh, Eric sat back down in the chair. "You've got my undivided attention."

"I've got to file some papers with the court." Cam snapped his briefcase shut.

"I'm betting these two fools are letting their dicks do their thinking about the cute blonde." Dylan shook his head. "Don't forget you've got hundreds of millions on the line, fellows. Maybe more if that platform gets damaged again. She might look sweet on a St. Andrew's Cross at Phase Four, but is it worth everything you've built?" The ex–CIA agent didn't wait for an answer, but headed for the back door.

After Dylan's exit, the only people left in the courtroom were Eric, Cam, and Scott.

"Let me know what you two decide about Megan Lunceford," Cam said and left them alone.

He and Eric watched as Cam walked away.

Then Eric said, "Convince me she's not our hacker."

He sat on the half wall, took a deep breath, and began. "Kip's skill as a programmer was quite good, which he loved touting to any who would listen."

Eric nodded. "I remember."

"But the only women he'd ever dated were definitely not MIT girls."

His brother chuckled. "You saying his wife is lacking in the brains department?"

Scott shook his head. "I remember the bimbos he brought to the Christmas party at the Dallas office, but he also dated that girl who was the psych major. Remember?"

"Wasn't her name Lila something?" Eric asked.

"I don't remember her last name. Kip preferred women with liberal arts degrees. For them to even get a second glance from him, they could have expertise in lots of things but not in programming. In TBK's first year, Vicky shamelessly flirted with him. We both know how that worked out for her."

"That's true. He cut her off at every turn."

"Okay, Mr. Logic, if all that's true, then how can Kip's wife be a programming genius that is able to get around all TBK's safety measures?" He watched Eric's eyelids narrow and brow furrow. "She might be an Einstein about art, music, history, or whatever, but not coding. Kip would've never married her if she was."

"Okay. I'm with you." Eric leaned forward as if to highlight what he was about to say. "She might not be the programmer behind the attacks on our system, but that doesn't mean she's not working with Kip or one of his associates."

His gut tightened. Eric was right. They couldn't just let Megan off the hook, no matter how much his feelings told him she was innocent. Someone might be manipulating her, convincing her to go along with his scheme with all kinds of promises.

"I've got an idea, bro," he told Eric.

"That's what worries me."

Ignoring the comment, he continued as the scheme became clearer in his mind. "We'll be able to keep an eye on her twenty-four hours a day, seven days a week. If she's involved in the hacking in any capacity, we'll discover it."

"Sounds too good to be true, which doesn't surprise me. You dream. I smash your dreams with reality. That's been our jobs at TBK and on the ranch. Details. What's your plan?"

Scott braced himself for Eric's reaction. "We'll offer her a job."

Eric looked like he was ready to explode. "Have you lost your fucking mind? She's the reason for TBK's current vulnerability."

"Best to keep our friends close and our enemies closer." As he laid out the rest of the plan for his brother, Scott vowed to himself to help Megan. Whatever it took, he would prove her innocence.

* * * *

Under the gray skies, Megan stood on the steps of the courthouse with her newly appointed attorney, Phoebe Blue. The woman's long dark hair, and shapely form seemed more suited for a career on fashion runways than in stuffy courtrooms. Phoebe's eyes fit her name perfectly. Pale blue and mesmerizing.

"We have a lot of ground to cover before next Tuesday, Mrs. Lunceford. Let's go to Lucy's and grab a bite. We can talk about your case over lunch."

Seven days in Destiny. Oh God. Her head was swimming with worry.

"Call me Megan, please," she requested, wondering how in the world she would be able to navigate the next week. Dread twisted her stomach into a pretzel of nerves.

Phoebe smiled. "It's a deal, Megan, if you promise to call me by my name, too."

"Of course," she agreed. "How long have you known the Knight brothers, Phoebe?"

"My whole life, but that won't be a problem. I'm working for you now. They're friends, but the law is the law and business is business. The court has ordered me to help you and that's exactly what I am going to do to the best of my ability."

Megan was relieved to have someone on her side, but still… "It's going to be a tough case, isn't it?"

"Very. Eric and Scott aren't the kind of guys to give up easily. I saw Dylan Strange behind them. I'm betting he's got some evidence that points to you."

"I'm innocent, Phoebe. I swear." She'd found it hard to look at the Knight brothers but couldn't resist a peek at the copresidents of TBK several times out of the corner of her eyes. She'd expected the Knights to be much older, like typical corporate billionaire moguls were. They weren't. She would guess them to be in their late twenties.

Eric was the one who seemed most comfortable in a suit and tie. Scott, as the judge had pointed out, was not so much. Eric's face was handsome, with chiseled features and a five-o'clock shadow, which highlighted his square jaw perfectly. Scott had the most beautiful lips she'd ever seen on any man. Eric's eyes were big, blue, and daring. Scott's were a rich chocolate color. Both had thick, finger-tempting dark hair.

Recalling the two billionaires' intensity and dangerous demeanors made her tremble again.

Phoebe's cell rang. "One second, Megan." She put it to her ear. "Hey, Ashley. You're already at the office? Good. Clear my calendar today and tomorrow. The Stone brothers and their fiancée were in the courtroom, too. I'm sure they'll understand why I have to delay getting their new wills finished for a couple of days. Great. I'll bring all her records with us after Mrs. Lunceford and I have lunch." Phoebe turned to her and nodded. "Tough case for sure, but I believe this client is well worth our best efforts. Okay. Bye." Phoebe tucked her phone back into her purse. "Ashley's my paralegal. I couldn't make it without her. Now, where were we?"

"I was telling you I was innocent."

Her attorney's eyes narrowed for a moment before widening. "I believe you."

"I can't tell you how much that means to me, Phoebe. I know Judge O'Leary assigned you to my case, but I have no money to pay you. I wish I did."

"Relax. I'll get a little compensation from the court. Not my normal hourly rate, but it will do. What do you think of Destiny so far?" Phoebe's tone sounded much like pride to her ears.

As they walked down the courthouse's front steps, Megan noticed the sky beginning to clear. "Just drove in right before court. I didn't have much time to take in the sights." *No credit cards. No money.* How was she going to make it until her hearing? She swallowed hard, but it didn't ease her anxiety.

"This must be your car," Phoebe said, stopping right in front of Granny Gremlin.

"It is, but how would you know that?"

"Small-town folks don't miss much." Phoebe peered inside. "Destiny has never had this kind of car on its streets before. That computer in the passenger seat is a real dinosaur. God, it is big. After lunch, I'll send someone to retrieve it. How long have you had this car, Megan?"

"She's not much to look at, but this old thing and I have been through so much together," Megan said. "That might be hard to understand."

"See my truck over there?" Phoebe pointed to a rusted Ford that had to be even older than Granny Gremlin. "My granddad gave that to me when I graduated high school. My brothers tease me all the time about keeping it, but I will never let it go. I understand better than most, Megan."

"I'm glad," she said, pleased that Phoebe was handling her case.

Phoebe crossed the street and began walking down the sidewalk. "You noticed the crowd behind us, didn't you?"

She nodded. "I was shocked to see so many people. There must've been other cases."

Phoebe shook her head. "Nope. Your case is the biggest buzz in Destiny right now. They'll all be there next Tuesday, too."

"I'm sure that most are on the Knight brothers' side." The whole audience would be against her. Phoebe was her only ally.

The beautiful attorney nodded. "They are local guys, so you're probably right."

"That's why I opted on a trial with a judge instead of a jury. Was that a mistake? Ethel seems very fond of the Knights."

"Most people are, Megan, but in Destiny people do the right thing. If you had chosen to have your case heard by a jury, those seated would've been fair, I'm certain. And Ethel's high ethics are unquestionable."

Then maybe she could count the judge as an ally, too. "That makes me feel a little better, but only a little."

Phoebe touched her on the arm. "I'll do my best for you, Megan. I can tell you're a very sweet person."

"Sweet but...?"

Phoebe turned the corner onto South Street. "But nothing. Sweet. Be honest and answer me this. Did you have anything to do with the hacking into TBK's systems? This is between client and attorney. It will go nowhere else. Trust me."

Her gut told her to trust Phoebe. With women, her gut was generally right. With men? Not so much. "I didn't do what Eric and Scott Knight are accusing me of. I swear it. I couldn't have done it because I'm a techno-idiot. I might be the only twenty-five-year-old in the world who still has trouble sending a text message."

"That'll be hard to prove." Phoebe pulled out a digital tablet from her purse. She touched the screen with her fingers. "Do you have a university degree?"

Megan shook her head. "I was only twenty when I married. After everything that happened, college wasn't feasible for me." She glanced over the lovely park in the middle of town, trying to recall what life had been like before meeting Kip and before her mother's illness. She'd been a sophomore at the University of Texas working on a degree in elementary education. Those days seemed several lifetimes ago, far away from the idyllic scenery of Destiny. "Your town square is beautiful."

"We call it Central Park. It's only one and a half acres. Everyone treasures it, but there has been a grassroots movement in the town to rename the park Destiny Square Park since I was a kid. The residents are pretty equally divided on the issue. My family belongs to the group that wants to keep the name the same, Citizens for Tradition."

Megan couldn't keep herself from smiling. "Sounds like quite a stir."

Phoebe paused as they came up to one of the strange statues that surrounded the park. "Make fun, but it's the one thing that divides this town during election time. Let's walk down to West Street. It'll give you a better look at the park. We'll come back to Lucy's in a sec." Her attorney pointed to the storefront on the southwest corner of the intersection.

"What are the people on the other side of the matter called, Phoebe? And what got everyone so up in arms about the name anyway?"

"They call themselves Destiny's Citizens' League. We call them Destiny's Opposition Group, DOGs, but only during campaign season and only in closed-door meetings." Phoebe continued walking down South Street. "The whole debacle began when the four dragon statues were commissioned as gifts for New York's Central Park by the residents here in 1978. It was meant as a token of camaraderie for the sister park."

The local politics in Destiny were clearly divisive and just as befuddling to her as any back home. Ahead next to the sidewalk they were on was one of the four rejected gifts Phoebe talked about. Megan was in awe of the work of art. It looked powerful, monstrous, and quite beautiful in an odd sort of way. "Why dragons?"

"Patrick O'Leary is the reason for that choice. He made the biggest donation. He wasn't a billionaire then, but he was pretty close."

She knew that name. "The judge's name was O'Leary, right? Ethel O'Leary?"

Phoebe nodded. "Patrick and his brother are married to her."

Her jaw dropped. "What? I don't understand. She's a bigamist?"

Phoebe laughed. "Not legally. I'm not sure which of the brothers she shares a marriage license with, but in her heart, she's married to both of them. That's quite common here in Destiny."

This seemed like such a normal place. "Apparently, there is more under the surface of your small town than I got from my first impression of it."

"Most definitely." Phoebe smiled and winked. "Destiny is home to a wide variety of eccentrics, freaks, weirdoes, and the unconventional. We're one of the most live-and-let-live communities in the country...well, except around election times."

Megan wished her neighbors back in Dallas were more open-minded like the citizens of Destiny. Five years since Kip's arrest in her mother's house hadn't softened a single disapproving glare from neighbors.

"Patrick is a brilliant man. He and Sam, his brother, built several successful multinational conglomerates together. They opened up markets all over the world, including China, India, Japan, Eastern Europe, and more. During his travels, Patrick became enthralled with local myths about dragons." Phoebe shook her head. "Whatever you do, don't ask him about it. He can talk about that topic for hours and hours. The truth is he believes they are real and still exist."

Megan laughed. "You're kidding."

"Nope. There are actually five dragons in town." Phoebe reached up beyond the base and patted the toe of the bronze dragon that was at least thirteen feet tall. "The fifth one is in front of the O'Learys' mansion and is much larger than its four cousins."

Megan smiled, wondering what it would be like to be able to have such childlike beliefs again. Not possible for her after all that had happened.

"This dragon is called The Green Dragon and is said to bring luck. Touch the dragon's toe, Megan. We're going to need a ton of its power next week if we have a prayer of beating TBK."

Her nerves exploded with renewed concern. "I'm not a big believer in luck."

"Me either, but as your attorney, my advice is for you to touch it anyway. It can't hurt."

"If it helps me beat the Knights, then I'm game." She placed the tip of her index finger on the toe of the bronze beast, doubting Tuesday's hearing would end well for her. Looking up at The Green

Dragon with its wings spread and its jaw agape, she noticed the image of a shamrock on its chest. "A little too precise, don't you think, Phoebe?" She pointed at the Irish symbol.

"O'Leary's parents came over from the Emerald Isle. Patrick will fill you in on all the details should you get to meet him. He really is a sweet guy." Phoebe led the way across South Street to the row of businesses on the other side. It reminded Megan of a train. "This first place is Phong's Wok. Another day I'll bring you here. Hiro Phong, the owner, has the best Chinese food you'll ever get between your chopsticks."

"Phoebe, do all the dragons have names?"

"The Blue Dragon sits on the southeast corner. We passed that as we were walking. Most of the women in Destiny call her Mother Dragon. She's said to safeguard the lives of women in labor. Black Dragon, also called Father Dragon, rests on the northwest corner of the park."

"You sound like you actually believe in these dragons." They crossed the street to Lucy's. "What's the other dragon called? The one on the northeast part of the park?"

Phoebe answered, "The Red Dragon."

That sounded ominous. "And its specialty?"

"Passion."

Yep. Ominous. "A love dragon?"

Phoebe nodded as they passed two other stores—Betty's Beauty Shop and Tara's Tea and Scones.

"Crazy names for businesses," she said.

"Agreed. That's Destiny for you." Phoebe opened the glass door of Lucy's. "Here we are."

Walking into the eatery, Megan's thoughts about her hearing pulled her back from the sweet, distracting tales of Destiny's dragon statues. Her troubles demanded her attention. Once again, her mind replayed the scene in the courtroom. Judge O'Leary seemed to be kind and even understanding, unlike her accusers, but that wouldn't help her make her case. Ten million dollars wasn't the issue. Just like the old saying about squeezing blood out of turnips, squeezing her funds wouldn't yield anything. Her house, the final gift from her mother, was the real issue according to what the judge had said.

How had she not realized it would also be at risk in all of this?

"Hey, Lucy." Phoebe waved to the middle-aged woman behind the counter dressed in a 1950s pink uniform with a little white apron and matching hat.

"Hey. Were you at the hearing? Surely it isn't over yet?" The waitress held a pitcher of tea in one hand and a Hula-Hoop in the other.

Megan couldn't imagine how the woman could serve food holding the classic ring.

Phoebe answered Lucy, "I was at the hearing and it is over."

Lucy called through the opening in the wall to what must've been the kitchen in the back. "Norman, lunch crowd will be on time."

A man's voice floated from the other side of the opening. "I'll be ready, baby."

"Phoebe, who is this?" Lucy asked.

"Megan Lunceford."

"Ah, the defendant." The waitress came around the counter and stepped up to Megan. Lucy's gracefulness was something to behold. She didn't spill a single drop of tea, even though she spun the Hula-Hoop in her other hand.

"The one and only," Phoebe answered. "Ethel postponed the hearing until Tuesday. Megan is my new client. Mind if we sit in one of the booths by the window?"

"Sure thing, Phoebe." Lucy turned to Megan. "I worked with your husband a while back."

This was the first person she'd ever met who knew Kip. "At TBK?"

"Yes. Eric and Scott recruited him from MIT. They were all in their early twenties. Me and Norm were the old farts. Still are but we're no longer at the company."

"Do you know if he had any family?" she asked, grasping for straws. If he did, maybe one of them might've gotten word about Kip's whereabouts, whether in prison or out.

"I don't think so, miss. He never mentioned any family. Kip was a smart guy. Very smart."

"Not too smart." Megan stopped short of saying more, unsure she should be sharing anything with the woman.

"I guess you're right considering all the shit that happened." Lucy pursed her lips for a moment before speaking again. "I know what he did, Megan. He's not out, is he?"

She shrugged. "I really don't know. I doubt it, though."

"Poor thing," Lucy said. "What a mess. You look like you haven't rested in weeks. What you need is a good, hot meal."

"I'm really not hungry," she lied.

"Nonsense." Lucy looked at Phoebe. "You and your client sit before the rest of the lunch crowd shows. Pour yourself some tea. I'll fix you two the special."

"Sounds great to me." Phoebe led her to the center booth by the window. "You like sweet tea or plain?"

"Plain," she answered, sliding into the blue vinyl seat.

"I'll be right back with our drinks." Phoebe left her alone.

The bell on the door to the eatery chimed. Several people she'd seen in the courtroom's gallery filed into Lucy's as expected.

Not wanting to meet their gazes, she looked down at her hands folded together on the table. Her world, what little was left of it, was hitting a new low. Megan had only thought she'd found the bottom that Kip's crimes had forced her down to. TBK's copresidents were going after her mother's house. Back taxes and overdue repairs were the least of her worries.

Phoebe came back with two glasses of tea. She set one down in front of Megan and then scooted into the booth opposite her. "You're going to love Lucy's burgers."

"I'm really not hungry, Phoebe," she said, knowing how low her funds were. No way could she pay for lunch. Her stomach growled in betrayal. She hoped Phoebe hadn't heard, but by the look on her attorney's face, she believed Phoebe must have. "Just the tea. Thanks." Her lack of funds presented a ton of challenges. One, food. Two, lodging. Three, transportation. Granny Gremlin would never make it back to Texas without a visit to a top-notch mechanic. Four, back taxes on her mother's house. Five, everything else.

Phoebe stared at her with understanding eyes. "I insist. You haven't lived until you've tasted one of Norm's creations." She reached across the table and squeezed her hand. "Megan, it's my treat."

Megan nodded. Phoebe had to know she was broke but was kind enough to not make her feel like a charity case, though that was what she was in truth.

Phoebe pulled out an iPad from her purse. "You mentioned working as a secretary. You must've worked on computers then."

"More of a receptionist, but yes, I have. The last job I had was in a dentist office. I kept the appointments and filed insurance claims." An image of the office manager's face at the place came into her mind. The woman had been sweet and apologetic, hating to have to fire her, but the policy was employees had to meet certain minimums from their credit history. Kip's black record had spilled over all her information, including her credit score of three hundred, the absolute lowest rating the three bureaus gave. She'd ended up on the bottom because literally everything had gone wrong.

Getting let go was something Megan had unfortunately become too familiar with.

"What about character references?" Phoebe asked. "Do you have anyone that we can get up here next Tuesday that would speak on your behalf?"

"No. It's just me." It had been that way since Kip's arrest and would most certainly be that way for the rest of her life. She didn't have any hope her future would be any different than now.

"Do you have any family, Megan?"

She looked out the large windows of the burger shop and gasped. Eric and Scott Knight were staring at her from across the street. A shiver shot up her spine. Only in Destiny for less than two hours and her whole world had turned upside down.

"No family. I'm alone."

Chapter Three

Eric gazed at Megan behind the big window of Lucy's. Their eyes locked for a moment. Suddenly, Megan turned her attention from him to Phoebe, who was sitting with her in the burger shop.

"Shall we make our offer to her or not?" Scott stood next to him on the sidewalk on the park side of South Street.

"I'm inclined to say 'not,' but I know you're not going to drop this."

His brother nodded. "You're right about that."

"You know she might refuse us," he said. Of the two of them, Scott was always quick to believe the best in people. Eric had been like him in the beginning of TBK. Not anymore. Not after Kip.

"I know." Scott removed the suit jacket and flipped it over his shoulder. "We have to convince her it's for the best."

"For whose best, bro? Ours or hers?"

His brother shrugged. "Maybe for all of us. Who knows?"

"Cam and Dylan are going to kill you for this. You heard them back there. Months of work will go down the drain if she agrees to this. They're certain she's guilty."

"Bullshit." Scott stared at him, continuing to make his case for the wacky scheme.

Keeping his eyes fixed on Megan behind the window, he half listened to Scott. Eric's attention was primarily on her, not his brother. Again, she peeked at him, their eyes locking for an instant. Even from here, he could see her cheeks turn red on her pale face before she looked back at Phoebe. If Megan was trying to be discreet, she was doing a terrible job of it. He couldn't help but grin at her awkward antics.

Scott's diatribe ended abruptly.

Eric turned to his brother. "What?"

Scott shook his head. "Tell me you actually believe that behind Megan's gorgeous green eyes is a maniacal criminal. She's innocent. You and I both know it."

"I don't know that." But his brother's point wasn't lost on him. She didn't seem capable of hacking into someone's personal laptop, let alone TBK's networks, which had some of the best security systems in the world. "Someone is getting past our firewalls and jacking with our code. If not her, then who?"

"Maybe Kip," Scott suggested. "We don't know if he's still being held or not, Eric. It's been five years. He might be using her to get to us."

That idea did have merit, though only a sliver or so. "He committed treason. I don't think you get out early for good behavior for that kind of crime."

"Well, let's find out what she knows about her husband's location, shall we?" Scott stepped into the street, heading to Lucy's and to Megan, a woman whose entrance into the courtroom had unsettled him.

Before that moment she'd run into the courthouse, Eric had been ready to bring her down. Now, he couldn't stop thinking about Megan. Her nervousness seemed to surround her every move in the hearing. How had Kip found such a sweet creature? More than that, how had the creep got Megan to agree to marry him?

He followed Scott across the street, hoping Megan would consider his brother's crazy proposal. The truth was, though he would never admit it to Scott or anyone, he wanted to learn more about the curvy blonde.

* * * *

Megan tensed as the door to Lucy's opened. The bell chimed the arrival of the two men who had forced her to Destiny in the first place. They were still in their suits, though Scott was carrying his jacket now. They both wore cowboy hats, which fit them perfectly.

Every table, booth, and barstool at Lucy's Burgers was taken.

"Here you go, ladies." Lucy set down two pieces of pie. "Your burgers will be up shortly."

"Dessert before lunch?" Megan asked.

"Sweetie, we don't follow any rules here in this town. Why not have dessert first and then your meal?" Lucy stepped back into the aisle between the booths and the tables and spun the Hula-Hoop around her waist, moving her hips to keep it from falling to the ground. The woman's figure was amazing. Lucy stopped her demonstration and placed the toy back in her left hand. "I've been having dessert before my meal for quite a long time, Megan. Look at me. I'm in the best shape I've ever been. Now, enjoy."

"Sounds good to me," she said, peeking over the woman's shoulder at Eric and Scott Knight. Her heart stopped. They were headed straight to her and Phoebe.

"The Knights are here," she whispered.

Phoebe turned her head to the guys' direction and then held out her hand to them. "Hold it right there, boys."

They didn't, which sent a new set of shivers through her. Why was she reacting this way to these men? Because when it came to men, she was always at a disadvantage. Case in point—she'd accepted Kip's marriage proposal after knowing him for only a blink of an eye.

"Hello, Phoebe," Eric Knight said, keeping his piercing blue stare fixed on Megan, not her attorney.

Scott Knight held out his hand to her. "Hello, Mrs. Lunceford."

Phoebe scooted out of the booth and moved right in front of the men, clearly trying to block them from moving closer. "I don't want you talking to my client. Whatever you have to say, you can tell me. I will convey it to her."

Phoebe was at least an inch and a half, maybe more, taller than her. The top of Phoebe's head came to the middle of the brothers' chests. They were six three at minimum, a full foot taller than Megan. They were giants, which made her feel even tinier.

Glad to be sitting instead of in Phoebe's place at the moment, she grabbed her fork, trying to ignore her sexy accusers. She would've done just about anything to be away from here—away from Eric and Scott Knight.

"We have an offer for Megan, Phoebe. Hear us out." Scott's voice reminded her of a summer breeze.

She was so tempted to look back at him but instead took a forkful of Lucy's apple pie. The bite exploded with sweet deliciousness in her mouth.

She closed her eyes, relishing the taste.

How long had it been since she had any real food? Days. She'd been living on chips and off-brand sodas for the whole trip. Before that, mostly ramen noodles.

Lucy was right about having dessert first. The filling of the pie definitely hadn't come from a can. This was homemade goodness through and through.

Famished, she took another bite, closing her eyes again. The luscious treat slid down her throat, warming her insides up and helping her body relax. God, she needed rest in the worst way. As she chewed on the yumminess with total abandon, exhaustion wrapped its sleepy fingers around every cell in her body. She and Granny Gremlin would need to find a place to hole up for the night. Shouldn't be hard to find in these rural parts.

"Megan, are you okay?" Phoebe asked, pulling her from her dreamy state.

She opened her eyes and saw three other pairs staring at her. Her cheeks flamed hot from embarrassment. Crawling under the booth's table seemed like a good idea at the moment.

"I'm fine," she said, noting how tiny her voice came out.

"You were moaning," Scott said. "Are you sure you're okay?"

Moaning? She placed the fork on the half-eaten pie's plate. Her pulse was racing in her veins. "Just eating Lucy's pie. It's delicious."

"We know." Eric's eyelids were narrowed. "We've had her pie. When was the last time you ate, Megan?"

Why was he asking her that? Was it to get more information to use against her next Tuesday? She wasn't about to give him what he wanted. "Should you and I be talking, Mr. Knight? Phoebe, didn't you just tell them to go through you?"

"I did, but I think his question is valid." Her attorney's eyes were filled with obvious concern. "You look like you're about to drop, Megan."

"Did you drive straight here from Texas?" Scott asked, sliding into the booth next to her.

The Knights were clearly used to people answering their questions and following their orders. They were billionaire moguls. Why wouldn't they? But she didn't work for them. Kip had. *Kip.* The male gender was a mystery to her. She was an idiot when it came to men, but no more. She'd steered clear for five years. These two weren't going to get her off track.

"That's none of you or your brother's concern. If you'll excuse me, I need to get something out of my car. Will you let me out?"

Scott didn't move, but remained so close to her she could feel the heat from his body. Eric did move, sliding into the booth opposite her and Scott.

Phoebe remained standing at the edge of the table, but her eyes never moved, remaining locked to Megan's. "Don't tell me you drove straight here in that sorry excuse of a car of yours?"

"Okay. I won't." Her nerves were frayed. Whose wouldn't be? The two men who wanted to take the only thing she had left in the world—her mother's house—were hemming her in. "Mr. Knight," she said to Scott. "Will you please move so I can get out of this booth?"

He shook his head. "You're about to drop, aren't you?"

"Scoot over, Eric," Phoebe said. When he did, she moved into the seat next to him. "From Dallas to Destiny has to be at least a fifteen-hour drive."

Megan didn't correct Phoebe that it was actually seventeen. She was already uncomfortable with all the attention she was getting from everyone. "I'm fine. Really I am."

"Everything okay over here?" Lucy placed two plates on the table. The smell of the enormous cheeseburgers made Megan's mouth water. The piles of shoestring fries next to each sandwich were just as tempting.

"No, it isn't." Megan's heart was thudding fast in her chest and her jitters and fatigue had mingled into a heady brew just shy of bravery but spot-on defiance. "These two men are bothering us. Can you have them removed from our booth, please?"

"I see," Lucy said with a grin and wink. "We might need to talk to Sheriff Wolfe. He's at the counter. Would you like me to get him, dear?"

The woman's mocking tone wasn't lost on her, but she didn't care. "Yes. Please." As Lucy turned to go to the local lawman, Megan looked at Phoebe. "Perhaps I should represent myself, Phoebe. You seem to be a little too chummy with these two."

Scott chuckled. "She's got fire."

"Guts, too." Eric's already-too-beautiful face became even more so when his manly lips curled up into the most mind-blowing smile she'd ever seen. He reached across the table and touched the back of her hand. "You need food and rest, Megan. We have an offer I think you'll like, but we can talk about it later. After."

"After what?" she snapped, pulling her hand into her lap. Why was she reacting so strongly to him, pushing him away? Sure, they were acting nicey-nice now, but what about the lawsuit? Eric and Scott were her enemies, not her friends. If what happened with Kip taught her anything, she knew there was only one person she could count on. Herself. Megan. No one else. Phoebe had been sweet, but that didn't mean a damn thing in the long run. Kip had been sweet, charming, and more. She would never forget how that turned out. Phoebe was not a friend. Eric and Scott were men, the gender she really would never trust again. Never, never, never.

Lucy walked up to the booth with the sheriff. "Your wish is my command. Megan, let me introduce you to our sheriff, Jason Wolfe."

"Order up," Norm called from the kitchen.

"Hold your horses, dear husband." Lucy filled hers and Phoebe's glasses. "I'll be back. Have more hungry patrons to take care of." The woman darted off, twirling her Hula-Hoop around her waist.

The sheriff stepped up to the booth. "What seems to be the trouble?"

Scott thrummed his fingers on the table. "We've got a woman who refuses to be honest, Jason."

Why were the Knights pushing this? What was their angle? She studied both of them.

Scott smiled at her, a broad grin that made his chocolate eyes even brighter, helping her warm to him even more. Of the two brothers, he looked much more approachable.

Eric's unhinging blue-eyed stare sent a hot shiver through her body. His intense gaze never left her. "We've got this covered, Jason."

She folded her arms over her chest, fighting the weariness inside her body. "Sheriff, you may remember me back in the courtroom. I'm Megan Lunceford."

"I know who you are, Mrs. Lunceford. Everyone in Destiny knows." The man turned to Phoebe, and their eyes locked in a way that seemed to show they had some kind of history, a painful one likely. After a few uncomfortable moments, Jason turned back to Megan. "She's your client, counselor. What do you say?"

Phoebe blinked and turned to her. "Megan, Eric and Scott are right about you. You're on the verge of collapsing, aren't you? Starving, too, I'm sure."

Megan's defenses were weak. Why should she trust any of them? Of course, she shouldn't. For whatever reason—overwhelming fatigue, crushing hunger, or staggering loneliness—the truth vibrated on her lips, but before the words came out, her eyes betrayed her, releasing sudden tears. She closed her eyes, ashamed for the outburst. She'd only cried in front of two people, besides her mother, in her entire life. The memory of that day when the two men rolled out the sheet-covered body of her mom from the hospital room called forth a new set of sobs. Damn her exhaustion for making her so weak, so open, so vulnerable.

Megan tried to tamp down her waterworks, but failed.

She felt an arm wrap around her shoulders, Scott's arm. "It's going to be okay, Megan. Trust me."

God, she wanted to, but how? Her instincts were worthless. History had proven that. Kip had verified, notarized, and filed that away. When it came to men, any men, she was mentally incompetent.

Fingers touched her cheek, Eric's fingers.

She opened her eyes and looked at his handsome face filled with what seemed to be concern. "I–I a–am so sorry about everything. God, I hate crying in front of people." Wiping her eyes, she turned to Phoebe. "You're right. I'm tired. Really tired. Please forgive me for my outburst."

"There's nothing to forgive, Megan." Scott pulled her into his muscled frame, and she couldn't resist. She leaned into him, enjoying the strength he was offering. "Eric, what do you say now?"

She looked at the other brother. A storm brewed behind those eyes that sent another round of shivers through her body.

Eric brushed the hair out of her eyes. "You don't have to worry about anything, Megan. We did this to you."

She shook her head. "No. You're not responsible for me."

"We are now," he said, turning back to the sheriff. "Like I said, we've got this."

"I think you do," Jason said. "I'll leave you to it then. Nice to meet you, Megan."

It was clear that she was the last person to be in charge here at the moment. No sense in asking the lawman to stay. He wouldn't. So, she answered, "You, too."

The sheriff turned to Phoebe. "Later."

"Bye." Phoebe's single syllable seemed laden with unspoken volumes from the past between the two. As Jason exited for his seat at the counter, Phoebe watched him.

Megan wondered what had happened that had caused the obvious rift. Maybe Phoebe didn't have good instincts about men either. She'd have to ask her about it one day. *One day?* How about seven? She shuddered, remembering why she was here in Destiny in the first place.

The Knights were suing her for ten million dollars. If she lost, they could even take the last thing left to her, her mother's home.

Pulling away from Scott, she took a deep breath and shook off the fogginess in her mind. She needed to think clearly and stay focused.

"Eat your lunch, Megan," Eric ordered in a tone that undeniably meant he didn't want any debate, only compliance. "Scott and I will talk with Phoebe about our offer to drop our lawsuit against you."

Had she heard him correctly or was her exhaustion and hunger now impacting her hearing? "Do you mind repeating that, Mr. Knight?"

"You're the one who asked us to go through your attorney, didn't you?"

She nodded.

"Okay. We'll give her the details about our offer."

"But you said something about dropping the case, didn't you?"

"Yes, I did."

None of this made any sense to her. She was Mrs. Kip Lunceford, despite her desire to get her marriage to the bastard annulled. Like everything else in her world, her funds had prevented her from pursuing a change to her marital status. Besides, she needed to know where Kip was being held, and the government wasn't forthcoming about those details. Not one damn bit.

Even with the little Megan had learned about Kip's time at TBK, she knew they had every right to hold a grudge. Kip had almost cost them their company, not to mention their freedom. How they'd been able to clear their names she had no idea. But they had. Here they were right in front of her, sexy flesh and hot blood.

She needed to rein her mind into control. "I've got to stop."

"Stop what?" Scott asked.

Had she spoken her inner thoughts aloud? She must have. She was more tired than she realized. "Stop wasting time and get to eating this delicious meal Norm made."

"I agree with you. Eat up, like Eric said." He sent her a smile, not the approachable kind she'd seen earlier. This one was hot and tempting. Scott's lips, so beautifully male, had likely ensnared many a woman. If she wasn't careful, they might do the same to her.

Scott and Eric left the booth. They walked to the counter where three seats had opened up.

Phoebe smiled. "Be careful with those two, Megan."

"Isn't that what I have you for?" She filled her fork with another bite of the delicious apple pie.

"We'll see what they have to say. I'll be right back." Phoebe walked to the brothers and took a seat between them.

Megan turned her attention to the cheeseburger. She took a bite and immediately knew Norm was a genius with ground beef. It was seasoned perfectly and so juicy, and she relished the flavors. Another bite and her hunger vanished. Why did this feel like a last meal of sorts? Because it most likely was. Luck never went her way. Whatever the offer, it wouldn't change her fate.

Watching the three talking gave her hope. The dream of better days sprung up inside her like a fountain, but she shoved it down.

This had to be some kind of trick or negotiating tactic by Eric and Scott. They might not get ten million from her, but they could get her mother's house. Even in its current state of disrepair it was worth just shy of two hundred thousand dollars. For billionaires, it probably wasn't much money, but it was some.

Why would Eric and Scott even consider dropping the case?

The answer was—*they wouldn't.*

Chapter Four

Eric kept his back to the counter at Lucy's, sitting opposite on the stool of what was expected from customers of the burger shop. He didn't care. Taking his eyes off Megan wasn't an option for him. Not now.

"Tell me what you have in mind for my client, guys." Phoebe was getting right to it. So like her.

The sheriff and his brothers still had it real bad for Phoebe, but none of the three would ever let on. Too bad for them, especially Jason. The breakup had been messy and unfortunately the talk of the town. Had it only been three years since Jason had arrested Shane, Phoebe's brother, landing him in prison for possession? One thing about Jason, he was a stickler for the rules. No way would he ever turn a blind eye to something illegal, even if doing his job meant losing his and his brothers' fiancée in the process.

"We want to drop the case." Scott was the worst poker player in Destiny, a total open book.

"Hold on, bro." Eric watched Megan gobble down her cheeseburger in a flash, proving to him how truly hungry she must've been. His brother was right. She was not the hacker. But someone was, and that someone had used her IP to get to TBK. That couldn't be good for her. "There's a stipulation. That's what we agreed on."

Scott cursed. "Damn it, Eric. You still can't believe she's guilty."

"I don't, but she might be in danger." When he saw Megan yawn, he had the oddest urge to run back to the booth, grab her up, and carry her to his bed—not for sex but for rest. The frail thing needed help, and whatever it took, he would do it.

Phoebe looked concerned. "What do you mean by 'she might be in danger'?"

"He's right." Scott took a sip of his iced tea. "We need to stick to the plan or she runs back to Texas and right into the crosshairs of whoever is using her to get to us."

"Exactly," Eric agreed. Mesmerized by every bite Megan took, he thought of about a dozen other things he wanted to do for her. Many of them had to do with seducing her out of her clothes. Who could blame him? She was gorgeous. Her body was a sheer delight for the eyes. But it was so much more than a one-time fling with her. His mind was turning over and over. Her need was so present and tangible to him, not just about money, of which clearly she had little if any, but also about trust. As a Dom familiar with teaching subs and new Doms about the life, he'd helped many find deeper and deeper levels of true intimacy. Trust meant something. Earning it meant even more.

Megan's suffering called to him like a siren's song. His urgency to comfort her, pleasure her, to give her all she needed was pounding inside him, inside his veins, inside his chest, pushing him to act. Sex with her was a part of it, but only a part. Trust. That was the crux of the matter and would take time. There was only one way to protect her from whoever was behind the attacks and also get to work on earning her trust—the plan Scott had laid out back in the courtroom.

"What damn offer are you talking about, guys?" Phoebe's irritation was growing. "Ethel assigned her to me. Unless you drop the case, my obligation is to her, not you. I know we're friends but I'm bound to keep her best interests in mind. Understand?"

Bound? God, he loved that word. Being a Dom was elementary to his character. The lifestyle gave order to a world that often hadn't made sense to him. Eric let his mind draw up an image of a naked Megan tied up in his favorite braided nylon rope. The red and black two-color combination would look so beautiful against her pale skin.

"We want to offer her a job," Eric said, keeping his eyes not on Phoebe but on *her*. "She becomes our personal assistant for three months."

"Make it six, bro," Scott interjected.

His brother was onto something. "A year is better." That should be enough time to win her over.

Scott smiled. "I'm all in with you on that one."

Phoebe stepped off the stool and stood in the aisle, blocking his view of Megan. "A year working for TBK? You'll drop the lawsuit?"

"Yes."

"You came up with this plan before you believed she was innocent, right?" she asked.

Eric nodded, shifting slightly so he could see past Phoebe to Megan. He didn't want her out of his sight.

Phoebe looked skeptical. "Neither of you answered my question about this danger thing. Enlighten me."

Scott filled her in on what Dylan had found about the digital breadcrumbs that led to her IP, to her house in Dallas. Someone was using Megan to get to the back doors Kip had left at TBK. Once they got what they wanted, she would be the one holding the bag. Most likely it was Kip's Chinese buddies behind it, and that could only mean she was on the radar of some deadly people.

"When she agrees to be our personal assistant for a year," Scott explained, "we can keep an eye on her."

"The deal is twenty-four seven, Phoebe," he added.

"Purely professional?" She held up her hand. "Don't answer that. I know you. She says 'no' to an invitation to your bedroom, you'll accept that. You want to keep her close, to protect her. I get it. Every unattached man in Destiny is ready to play white knight for a woman in trouble." Phoebe sighed and glanced for a microsecond at Jason. Apparently, she still had it bad for him, too. "What happens when the real criminal is brought to justice? What then? You send her on her way back to Texas?"

He couldn't imagine letting Megan go, but what choice did he and Scott have? She wasn't from Destiny. She didn't know their ways.

Most outsiders thought that a family consisted of one man and one woman. More than one man sharing one woman was unthinkable. But he and Scott had grown up expecting the same kind of life their parents had shown them. Two dads and one amazing mom.

"What would you have us do?" he asked.

Phoebe shook her head. "Don't break her heart, guys. Please. She's a frail little thing."

"We won't." Scott spoke first. "I'm already gone on her, and by the way Eric is acting, it's clear, so is he."

"Fine. But I'm going to recommend she holds for a three-month contract, not twelve."

"Why?" Eric moved his attention to Phoebe. "Have you not heard a single word we've said?"

"I have, but you two need to get off your asses and help her. Three months is more than enough time to figure out who is behind the hacking."

Eric's gut tightened. "It took Dylan nearly a year to discover what he did, and you expect us to finish the job in three months."

"Actually, I hope sooner. I agree, she needs help and protection. If the Knight brothers want to give it to her, then I'm all for it."

"Glad to know you're on our side on this one," he said.

"I'm not. I'm on Megan's side. That's all." Phoebe looked like an overprotective sister. "You wrap this up, guys. Three months is more than enough time to get the bad guy. And if she falls in love with you and you do send her back to Texas, she has more of a chance of healing from the end of a ninety-day fling. Longer, I'm not so sure."

"Is this about Jason and you or about Megan?" Scott asked. He was always the open book.

"Screw you, Scott Knight." Phoebe turned on her high heels and marched to Megan's booth.

"That went well," Scott said.

Eric watched as Phoebe told Megan about their offer. "Fuck. Three months. It's not enough time, Scott."

"Time to find the hacker or time to get Megan to fall in love with us?"

"Maybe both. I don't know. But our first priority has to be finding the hacker."

"I agree, bro," Scott said. "We're going to have to be patient with her."

His dick definitely wasn't on board with that part of the plan. He was hard just looking at her. What would he be like when the most beautiful creature he'd ever seen in his life was with Scott and him twenty-four seven?

* * * *

Megan couldn't believe what Phoebe was telling her. "They can't be serious."

"I can assure you, they are." Phoebe took a bite of her meal.

"No lawsuit and Eric and Scott Knight are offering me a job. Why?" It didn't make any sense.

What was it about these men that mesmerized her so? They were mouthwateringly handsome, for sure, but that wasn't the entire reason.

"It's a good offer. There's little chance we can beat their charges next Tuesday." Phoebe reached across the table and took her hand. "You want to keep your house?"

As her heart seized a tiny bit, she nodded.

"Take their offer. They also think you're in danger, Megan."

"Where do they think this supposed danger is coming from?"

"Great question. You'll have to ask them yourself." Phoebe raised her hand and motioned the Knight brothers their direction.

Megan's cheeks were on fire and her belly swarmed with butterflies. "Why did you do that?"

"I've done my duty as your attorney, Megan. Time for you to make a decision."

Of course, Phoebe was right, but how could she agree to such an obvious illicit proposal? Twenty-four hours a day, seven days a week clearly meant she would be residing in their house. It didn't take a genius to figure out what duties they would expect, despite what Phoebe had assured her. Apparently to the Knight brothers, employee benefits ran straight to the bedroom. As much as she didn't trust them, even more, she didn't trust herself around them. Given her past record, it made a lot of sense to be skeptical and keep her guard up.

The billionaires scooted into the booth, this time with Eric taking the seat next to her. Scott moved in next to Phoebe.

Eric spoke first. "What do you think of our offer, Megan?"

Her intuition kept screaming they were good men, ready to help her. But discernment clearly wasn't a skill she'd mastered. "Let me make sure I get this straight. You want to hire me as a personal assistant for you and your brother."

"That's right."

"I'll be on the clock day and night, seven days a week, with no vacation, no breaks."

He nodded.

"In exchange for this, TBK will drop the lawsuit against me."

"Yes."

"Three months only?"

Eric frowned. "I'd like a longer commitment from you, Megan."

Phoebe leaned forward and pointed her index finger at him. "I already told her you would settle for three months. Don't push me, Eric Knight."

He looked annoyed with the attorney. "Okay. Three months, Megan. Will you do it?"

"I'm not sure about this. If you think I'm in danger, you must know I'm innocent. Why not just drop the lawsuit and be done with this mess once and for all?"

He leaned in. "Because I'm not done with you, Megan Lunceford." His tone was throaty. "Be honest with us, you're completely broke, yes?"

That was none of his business. "If I am, what difference does that make to you?"

He slapped the table, causing an electric-like tremble to shoot through her entire body. "A whole helluva lot of difference, baby, is what it means to me."

"Chill, bro. Don't be a bastard. You're scaring her." Scott leaned forward across the table. "Don't worry, Megan. You'll get used to Eric's argumentative, demanding, and contrary side in time. It's only a percentage of his larger-than-life character. He can be quite charming and kind when he needs to be. You'll see."

She'd seen glimpses of that part of Eric's supposed character moments ago before heading to the counter to tell Phoebe about their job offer. "That's why I'm worried about your offer. I'm still a married woman."

"Let me calm your nerves," Scott said, though his brother's face seemed to darken with some internal storm. "We want you here with us until we figure out who was using your IP to hack into our systems. We also want to make sure no one has access to your house."

"What? My house?" The shock of that statement nearly had her on her knees. "You think Kip might be out already? That he's been in my home without my knowledge?" That possibility had her shivering with dread.

"Could be." Scott looked at her two empty plates. One had held her cheeseburger and fries, and the other the delicious pie. "You want more?"

"No. I'm full to the brim," she said honestly.

Eric touched her elbow, sending a tantalizing shiver through her. "You haven't been in contact with your husband recently, have you?"

"No. Only a few letters since the FBI removed him five years ago. I've tried to find out where they took him but have come up short. I have no idea where he is."

"Do you care to know?" Eric's tone made her uncomfortable.

Why was he probing her for answers? Did he still suspect her of wrongdoing despite what he'd told Phoebe, despite this get-out-of-lawsuit-free card they were dangling in front of her, despite everything?

Her gut told her the Knights were okay. They could be trusted. Should she tell them that she only wanted to find Kip to serve him annulment papers? She wasn't sure what the right thing to do was, so she kept that little bit of information to herself. In time, should her intuition about the guys turn out to be correct—though that would be a first for her—she would tell them then. Not until.

"He's my husband. Of course I want to know where he is."

Eric's mouth twisted slightly before he removed his fingertips from her elbow. "Know this, Megan. Whoever is behind the hacking didn't have to be in your house. They could've jumped on your modem wirelessly from a car parked more than a block from it. You don't need an MIT degree to do that."

"But having one wouldn't hurt, would it?" She knew Kip had that degree. Or at least he'd told her he did.

Scott pulled out a pen from his jacket and took one of the white paper napkins from the dispenser on the table. He wrote something on it and slid it over to Eric. "Good?"

"Whatever she wants, bro. Whatever it takes." Eric pushed it in front of her. "How's this for your starting salary, Megan? Will this work for you?"

She looked down at the number and her jaw dropped. "I don't know what you two think I'm willing to do for this, but you better figure out real quick that there are some things I won't do."

Phoebe took the napkin and chuckled. "Damn, boys. Billionaires or not, have you lost any sense of what this kind of money means to most people?"

"I don't understand," Scott confessed.

Phoebe pushed the napkin back to her. "Talk about overshooting the mark. Any woman with half a brain would be scared out of her mind with this many digits on a napkin. Trust me, Megan has more than her fair share of brains."

"I can't accept this. It's unbelievable."

Eric leaned forward. "Look at me, Megan."

Unable to resist, she turned to him and gazed into his blue eyes.

"Being our personal assistant doesn't mean we expect anything you don't want to do. Whatever limits you have we will respect. It's a job. Plain and simple. You want the truth. We believe you are in danger. Someone with knowhow got through the best cyber security systems in the world to get to our code, code that would garner a small fortune from certain interested parties. Having you by our side will help us find them. You are safe and our code is protected. Win-win."

Unable to move her eyes off the figure on the napkin, she laughed nervously. "It's too much. I can't accept this kind of money from you. I don't have a college degree even."

Scott handed her the pen. "Tough negotiator. Impressive. Write down the amount you would agree to, Megan."

She laughed. "Three months. That's all. I want to trust you guys."

"Then trust us," Eric stated firmly.

"You see why I'm the spokesperson for TBK. My brother is too blunt and harsh. I, on the other hand, am warm and open."

"That's one way to describe you, bro. I can think of another."

"See what I mean, Megan?"

Their brotherly banter was endearing and sweet. They clearly cared for each other deeply.

"Make your case, gentlemen," Phoebe suggested. "You have my client on the ropes. Seal the deal."

Scott sent her a knowing wink. "Eric and I can be trusted, Megan. We're animal lovers, for heaven's sake."

"I'm betting horses are your favorites based on your choices of hats. Stetsons, right?"

The Knight brothers laughed, which felt like magic to her ears.

She turned to Eric. His face had softened a bit, making him look even more appealing.

"Dogs and cats, too, sweetheart," he said jokingly. "We love all God's creatures."

"Maybe so, but you still could be playing me, Eric, lover and defender of all four-legged creatures," she said, hitting with her own dose of teasing but with a dash of truth mixed in. "It's the two-legged variety that has me worried. In particular, my two legs, if you catch my drift."

Phoebe shook her head. "Like I said, this girl is sharp."

"She's going to keep us on our toes, that's for sure." Scott sent her a toothy grin. God, the man was devastatingly good looking.

Eric's tone turned serious. "Trust me, Megan, in the Knight house, the word 'no' means no. You have nothing to worry about."

His words eased some of her worries. "Phoebe, you know these guys, right?"

"My whole life."

"Should I trust them?"

"Yes, but my legal advice is to keep one eye open at all times." Phoebe smiled. "Gentlemen, yes. Devils, definitely."

Her heart was thudding in her chest. Could her troubles be a thing of the past once she said "yes" to the Knights' offer? Was it really that simple?

She scratched out the six figures Scott had written down on the napkin. "I don't want to be a charity case for you. I want to earn my way, fair and square."

"That works for me," Scott said. "You've been a secretary. A personal assistant needs the same kind of qualifications as that."

"What's your number, Megan?" Eric's patience was without a doubt fading.

"Hold your horses, boys." Lucy stepped up to the booth. "Give the girl time."

Had Lucy been listening the whole time? Apparently so. Looking around the other booths and tables near theirs, Megan realized with all the heads turned in her direction that minding one's own business didn't seem to be the rule in Destiny.

For the first time in her life, she didn't really care. What was it about this place that had gotten to her? It wasn't the place at all. It was the people. They seemed so genuine. From Judge Ethel, to Sheriff Jason, to Lucy, to Phoebe, and yes, to even Eric and Scott—especially Eric and Scott.

She closed her eyes, trying to come up with a reasonable figure. Three months of work. The most she'd ever made was at the dentist office. That would be her starting point. She opened her eyes and wrote down the hourly rate she'd received there—twelve dollars and fifty cents. Multiplying it by twenty-four hours a day for ninety days, she came up with the mind-blowing amount that would pay the back taxes on her mother's home and give her enough money to start her life over.

"Twenty-seven thousand dollars is my counter, take it or leave it. Your call, guys."

"Done." Eric nodded and held out his hand for her to take.

She did and they sealed the deal.

Scott shook her hand, too. "We just saved ourselves over one hundred thousand bucks, bro. That's got to be the best bargain we've ever made."

"Agreed." Eric left the booth and stood at the end of the table. "Time to earn your paycheck, Megan."

Her jaw dropped. "Now?"

He smiled. "Right now. We need to get you settled into your room at our house. Where are your things?"

"You love to bark orders, don't you, cowboy?" Phoebe asked.

He frowned. "Your services are no longer required for her."

"That's not your call, Eric. Besides, I like Megan. I wouldn't mind having a smart woman like her as a confidant and advisor." Phoebe grabbed her hand and squeezed. "What do you say? Buddies?"

She nodded, glad to have a new friend.

Scott got out of the booth and to his feet. "I'm with Eric on this one. Let's get you settled into our house first. Then we can move on to the next part of the day."

"House? Your house?" Phoebe mocked. "Call it by its proper name. The Knight Mansion."

"We've never dubbed it that," Scott said.

"Maybe not, but everyone in Destiny has. Don't forget, Megan." Phoebe winked. "One eye always open with these two."

"I won't."

"Enough. Let's get going," Eric stated flatly, but his eyes twinkled with what seemed to her as satisfaction. He liked to win, most definitely. But she'd won, too.

"Okay." She stepped out of the booth and the Knights surrounded her. They towered over her, making her feel so very tiny and feminine. "All my stuff is in my car."

The lawsuit was off the table. She wouldn't have to sleep in her car for the next seven days. Her stomach was full. Things were looking up, even though her future as their personal assistant seemed unclear. What would she be doing for them, really? Taking notes? Making appointments? Screening their calls? All of the above and more?

"Lead the way, sweetheart." Eric's deep, commanding tone made her deliciously dizzy.

The only way to find out was to take the first step.

When he put his arm around her, she thought her knees would buckle.

They didn't, thank God.

Three months wasn't so long. Whatever happened, she would survive. She always had. She would again. At the end of her contract to them she would have twenty-seven thousand dollars. Nine thousand would go to the back taxes, saving her house from being seized and auctioned off by the county. She would use another five thousand of the remainder to make much-needed repairs for the home. And she would splurge on one thing. She'd throw out the futon, which had been her only place of rest since Kip's arrest. Then she'd get herself a real bed, queen-size.

They walked out the door of Lucy's. "What about the computer you were supposed to bring, Megan?" Eric asked. "Where is it?"

"With everything else I own, Mr. Knight. In my car." Her words came out sharper than she'd meant them to. Her nerves were shot and apparently her tongue was taking advantage of that.

Suddenly, Eric stopped. "Careful, Megan. I expect a certain level of courtesy and respect from my assistant. Understand?"

"Yes, Sir. I'm sorry. Just tired."

What had she really gotten herself into agreeing to the Knight brothers' contract?

Chapter Five

The Knights' address was Number Three, O'Leary Circle, Destiny, Colorado.

Awestruck, Megan walked between Eric and Scott along the gorgeous walkway up to their home.

Phoebe had been right. This wasn't a house—this was a mansion. It was massive enough to house ten families, not just two brothers. And it was just one of three unique-looking estates on this most exclusive street in Destiny. In fact, O'Leary Circle didn't have any other homes on it.

Eight marble two-story columns created a most impressive front to the structure. "What style is this?"

Eric rolled his eyes. "Now you've gone and done it, sweetheart."

"What?"

"Scott fancies himself an expert in architectural history." Eric offered her his arm as they walked up the steps to the massive wooden doors.

"Don't listen to my Luddite brother. Architecture has a far greater impact on society in the long term than sculptures, paintings, even music. Master architects give us the places to work, play, and raise our children. Our lives are spent in their designs. What they do matters."

"I see what you mean," she said to Eric. "He's passionate. Scott, my mother's house is perfect for me but I'm sure no master architect designed it."

"What kind of house is it?" Scott asked.

"Simple. Ranch style. One floor. Built in 1962. Nothing like yours."

"Most likely your mom's home has influences of several masters in its design. For instance, Joe Eichler made the ranch home widely available when he developed huge housing tracts for returning vets of World War II who could buy a home using the GI Bill."

Megan nodded, recalling the day she and her mother had been visited by the very first owner's widow. The woman had knocked on the door, asking if she could tour the house one last time. Her mom had welcomed her in with open arms. Megan had listened to the elderly lady share stories about her husband for over an hour. After the woman had left, her mom had taken the time to remind Megan, age seven then, to treat seniors with respect. Always. So many life lessons her mother had given her. God, she missed her every day.

"Enough, bro." Eric opened the double ancient wooden doors. "Let's get our new assistant settled in before you start another lecture about Frank Lloyd Wright, Louis Kahn, or Andrea Palladio."

"My God, you actually do listen."

"Until my ears bleed, bro."

Megan laughed. The brotherly ribbing was sweet. "What kind of style is your place?"

"It's a modern interpretation of a sixteenth-century Italian Renaissance style," Scott answered as they stepped into the foyer of the mansion.

Her jaw dropped. Their entry was as big as her mother's entire home. Twenty feet above her head was a dome that acted as the ceiling to this space. In the center of it was a round skylight that let the sun in. On the walls were paintings that must've cost more than ten homes like her mom's.

"Follow me," Eric instructed, and of course, she did.

As they headed up the stairs, she moved her eyes over the incredible home. She'd known that Eric and Scott were rich, but this place was way beyond a run-of-the-mill millionaire's home. Of course, they were billionaires, so it made sense. Down a hallway, she looked to her right and saw an oak-paneled library with a beautifully carved plaster ceiling, stained-glass windows, and a large stone fireplace. Elegant yet masculine. It suited them.

They turned a corner and another door was open. The room beyond was painted black, and in the center of it was a contraption she couldn't identify, not quite a table but not quite a bench either. When she saw the items on the table next to the strange thing, her breath caught in her chest. *Sex toys?* Three of them were shaped like giant penises.

The only things that had helped her through the last five years had been her romance novels. She and her mother had read sweet ones together during her chemo sessions. Megan discovered much hotter ones after Kip's arrest that spoke to her on both a romantic and erotic level. She devoured book after book, enjoying a wide variety of erotic romance stories—ménage à trios, sex toys, and yes, even BDSM. But reading and doing were two entirely different things.

"You're curious, aren't you?" Eric said with a wicked grin.

She shook her head and looked down at her feet, hoping he couldn't read her mind. Were Eric and Scott like some of the men in the books she loved? Her heart pounded hard in her chest, and she felt tingly all over.

Eric cupped her chin, gently pressing her to look up. She did. "I told you not to worry, Megan. Remember?"

"Yes, but—"

"But nothing. You never have to go into this room or even think about it." He reached over and shut the door to the naughty space. "Whatever you need, Megan, that's what you'll get from us. Understand?"

"I guess so." Kip had worked for Eric and Scott. Why would he choose to steal from them? So far, they'd been generous and kind to her. Was there another side to the Knight brothers she had yet to see? Recalling her wedding night, she bet there was only one person responsible for the crimes. Kip only cared about Kip. The bastard was a total user. Nothing more. Once the three months were over, she would have the money to hire the right attorney—maybe Phoebe—to finally get her marriage annulled even without Kip's signature. *Be Your Own Lawyer* was a book she'd gotten from the library that mentioned grounds she could use. Abandonment. The FBI could keep Kip under ice for as long as they wanted.

Scott looked at her with the sweetest stare she'd ever seen in her life. It worked to tamp down her worry. "Bro, cool it with the Big Bad Dom act, okay? She's our guest."

Eric released her chin. "Good enough for now. Later? A guess won't suffice, but you're exhausted and need rest."

At the end of the hall, they came to a door where the man who had sat behind the brothers in the courtroom was changing its knob. Even though indoors and on the floor here, the guy had on shades and was wearing a suit and tie.

"Is the light too bright in here for you?" she asked him.

Eric laughed. "God, I love your sass. His Aviators are just a part of his signature look, Megan."

"All done, buddy." The man stood and placed his tools in the box next to him. Then he handed a set of keys to Eric.

Eric took them and nodded. "Great. Megan, let me introduce you to Dylan Strange. He's a friend. He's also put a lock on your door as well as a deadbolt." Eric handed her the keys. "These are for you."

Scott turned to her. "We meant it when we said we want you to feel comfortable in our home."

"Thank you." She took the keys and curled them up in her hand. Eric and Scott deserved their gallant surname. She turned to Dylan. "It's nice to meet you, Mr. Strange."

The man's eyes narrowed at first. Then he extended his hand to her. "And you, Mrs. Lunceford."

She shook his hand.

"Enough with the introductions," Eric stated. "Megan needs rest."

Dylan nodded. "I've got an early flight in the morning, so I'll be saying my good-byes now."

Eric waited until Dylan was gone. "The bathroom in this suite already has a lock. No one will disturb you. Scott and I will have Gretchen unpack your things."

A sudden flash of foolish jealousy shot through her. "Gretchen?"

"A person we cannot live without. Gretchen Hollingsworth keeps this house running."

"Yes, I do, sir," a silver-headed woman said in a distinctive British accent. Megan guessed her to be in her mid-sixties. "And with little or no help from you two lads."

"How many times do we have to ask you not to wear that outfit?" Scott hugged the lady.

The formal maid uniform was light gray with a crisp white apron. Gretchen smiled, making her green eyes sparkle like emeralds. "I believe that employed domestics, whether maids or manservants, should wear uniforms, Mr. Scott. I've told you that a thousand times."

"This isn't *Downton Abbey*, Gretchen, and you're much more than a maid to us."

"Employment as a domestic is, I believe, an honorable profession. I'm proud of my uniform." The lady sent her a quick wink. "And how would you know, Scott, if this is or isn't *Downton Abbey*? Whenever I turn my television show on in the den, you head for the exit every time."

"Enjoy your soap opera all you want," Scott said. "How would you say it?" He continued in a terrible attempt at an English accent, "Not my cup of tea."

Gretchen shook her head. "Every male needs to leave this space right now."

Scott saluted and Eric leaned down and kissed the sweet woman's cheek.

"Go, before I get a broom to your behinds." They marched off, and Gretchen turned to her. "Welcome to Knight Mansion, Mrs. Lunceford."

"Please call me Megan."

"You Americans and your informality." Smiling broadly, Gretchen led her into the most luxurious bedroom she'd ever seen. "I'll draw you a warm bath and then I'll put away your things, dear."

"Thank you, Gretchen." A castle, two handsome Knights, and Gretchen. What woman wouldn't feel like a princess?

* * * *

Scott's pulse pounded hard in his veins as he and Eric walked down the hallway away from Megan's room—away from Megan, who was with Gretchen. "Want a drink?"

Eric shook his head. "I need my thoughts clear."

"Agreed."

There was no doubt about Megan's innocence anymore for either of them. Eric was clearly on board, too. The little time with her had been proof enough. She was kind, honest, and the most beautiful creature in the world.

When they got to the door of the library, Eric stopped. "This is a fucked-up mess."

"We have a lot to figure out, bro." Scott closed his eyes, hoping to find the way through this horrible maze. "We've got to help her."

"Dylan's evidence means one thing—someone was using Megan's IP from her mother's home to get into TBK's network." Eric's tone might be steady, but he knew his brother better than anyone. A storm was clearly brewing under the surface of all that calm.

Scott opened his eyes. "You think it's someone from the inside?"

"Maybe, but the viruses have Kip's fingerprints all over them. I found ten lines in the fucking hack's code that were identical to what we found when he sold the targeting software to the Chinese back then. Fuck. This is bad for her."

He agreed. Déjà vu was crashing in on them. Ten months ago,

they'd cracked a flaw in the government's drone guidance systems and had won an enormous contract to fix it. "What are we missing? It's got to be right in front of us."

"Five million lines of code in and the first backdoor attack came. After that, three more a few months apart from each other." Eric was in that space of his where he was working out all the variables and outcomes.

"I've run it over and over in my head. This hacker is only testing us. The contamination isn't their endgame." The last attack had been three months ago. The best and brightest from the CIA, FBI, and even TBK had put in the best security systems on the network. He and Eric believed, despite all the good feelings the team had, another was coming. If unprepared and not ready for the hacker's next attack, the entire project would be scrubbed and the code would be destroyed. They'd end up losing the government contract. How long would they continue to pay for their mistake in trusting Kip?

Eric sighed. "Let's head to the basement. Target practice will clear our heads."

"Great idea, bro."

Their basement had four distinct spaces. One was a theatre room with the latest and greatest screening equipment. Another was a wine room for their collection. To the left of that one was the game room—pool table, wet bar, pinball games, and card tables. The space they were headed to was the gun range, their favorite place to think and chill. The soundproofing had cost a small fortune but was well worth the expense.

After unloading several clips into the targets, Scott removed his ear protection and motioned for his brother to do the same.

"You've got something?" Eric asked.

"Maybe the techs will pull something from her computer that will be useful to us. But I'm thinking her modem might still have some digital breadcrumbs on it."

"Hell yeah it could." Eric slapped him on the back. "That's using the old noggin."

"We could have someone from the Dallas office retrieve it for us. Vicky even. She's the lead down there."

Eric shook his head. "No way. Have you forgotten she had the biggest crush on Kip back then?"

"Yeah, but I can't believe she's a mole. Remember how shocked and disgusted she seemed after learning of Kip's betrayal of TBK?" Vicky had been with them since the beginning. If they couldn't trust her, whom could they trust? But Scott wasn't ready to test that yet. "What about Felix? He's there, too. He could help."

"I know we've checked and rechecked everyone's background, but it's not enough." Eric was obviously not ready to trust anyone but him completely.

Scott felt the same way. Kip's betrayal had changed them both. "We've also verified the contamination came from outside the system."

"We have, but until we catch the motherfucking hacker, it must be one of us. Megan deserves that much." Eric paused. "I think that I'm the obvious choice."

Scott nodded. "There's no one I trust more, bro."

Eric sprinted up the stairs. "Since we were going to use the plane for the New York meeting, Josh probably can have it ready to take off within the hour for an unscheduled Dallas trip." Josh was a friend and TBK's lead pilot.

Scott raced behind Eric. "I'll call the O'Learys and see if we can use their plane tomorrow."

"Exactly. I'm sure they won't mind. Let's not tell Megan where I'm going, okay? We don't want her to worry."

"Agreed."

They came to the top of the stairs and found Gretchen. Beside her was one of Eric's pieces of luggage. "I took the liberty of packing for you."

"How did you know?" Scott asked. Gretchen seemed to always be several steps ahead of them, whatever the challenge.

"Considering Megan's situation and how you two already feel about her, I knew one of you would stay with her to be her bodyguard and one would charge off into the night to get the jump on whatever danger is stalking her. I had a fifty-fifty chance of picking correctly on the division of tasks. Pretty good odds."

Scott grabbed her hands and squeezed. "Better than fifty-fifty, right?"

She tilted her head to the side and winked. "I'll never tell."

"Thank you." Eric kissed her on the cheek.

"You're very welcome. Now, go." She turned to Scott. "I'll get your bags ready for the meeting in New York. You're still going, correct?"

He nodded, wondering how they'd ever survived without the amazing woman.

"Eric, go," Gretchen said firmly. "I'll take care that Scott and Megan get off tomorrow with a hot breakfast and both their bags packed for the meeting in New York."

"We need to leave here no later than four," Scott said. "You don't have to get up that early."

Gretchen smiled. "Don't worry about me. It will be nice to have the house to myself for a change. I'll cover things here. You both have work to do to help your lady."

"She's not our lady, Gretchen." Eric's words might be true but they were filled with something he'd never heard from his brother before. Eric was as interested in Megan as he was, but they both knew that being interested and actually winning her were two different things.

"Poppycock. I've never seen you two in this state before with any woman, and the saints and I all know there have been plenty of trollops traipsing through this place over the years. You're in love."

"We only just met her." Scott put his arm around the sweet woman. "You're a hopeless romantic."

"Trust me. In seventy-eight years I've forgotten more than you two will ever learn."

"I'll confess that I've never met anyone quite like her before," Eric said. Then his eyes widened. "I can't believe it."

"What?" Scott asked.

His brother placed his hand on Gretchen's shoulder. "In the seventeen years you've worked for our family, you've never told us your age before."

Her jaw dropped. "If you tell a soul, I swear on me parents' graves I'll make you pay dearly."

Eric kissed her again. "I wouldn't dare. Besides, you look twenty years younger than your actual age."

"That's enough of that, young man." Gretchen's cheeks were actually red. "Now be off with both of you. Megan needs you two at your best. Go get the bad guy."

"I will." Eric rushed out the door, heading to Walden-Jackson County Airport, which was over an hour from Destiny.

Living in the Rockies had so many advantages, but the one disadvantage was the lack of flat land to build airports. Walden-Jackson was the closest to them. He and Eric were working to get a single runway private airport built on one of the few pieces of acreage in all of Swanson County that would work for the project. The stretch was at the lowest elevation of the Stone Ranch and bordered the Steeles'.

He and Gretchen said their good-nights, and he went to his room. He pulled out his cell. It was still early, just after 5:00 p.m. This time of year with daylight savings in play, the sun didn't set until after eight.

He clicked on Patrick O'Leary's number.

"Hello," his neighbor said.

"Hello, Patrick. This is Scott Knight."

"Got the caller ID, lad. I know 'tis." Patrick's slight Irish brogue always made Scott smile. It got heavier whenever the man was tired or after a few drinks.

"I have a favor to ask."

"This about Mrs. Lunceford?"

"Yes. Eric and I believe she's in trouble. She's clearly innocent, Patrick."

"That she is. Pretty, too. What can I be doing for ya?"

He told him about Eric taking TBK's jet to Dallas and about the meeting in New York.

"Don't say another word, Scott. Take ours. I'll call the pilot. What time do you want him ready to go?"

"We'll leave Destiny at four."

"Done. I'll tell the pilot five thirty. Your brother and you be careful."

"We will. Thanks, Patrick." Scott clicked off his phone and put it on the charging station on his desk.

He stripped off his clothes and climbed into his lonely bed, hoping to get a little shut-eye before Gretchen knocked on his door in the morning. But he knew it wasn't going to happen even after the sun went down.

Images of Megan whirled in his head like a kaleidoscope.

The first moment he saw her with the papers falling to the courtroom floor appeared. Then came the memory of her sitting at the defendant's table next to them, her hands trembling, followed by sitting with her in the booth at Lucy's. Walking next to her into his and Eric's home. Leading her past the playroom and seeing her eyes widen in obvious surprise and a tinge of curiosity.

Every moment with her felt special and potent.

But she was still married to Kip. Did she still love him? Why hadn't he bothered to ask her that?

Tomorrow he would make sure he found out.

Chapter Six

Megan found herself rested and nervous. Odd combination, but true.

Waking to Gretchen's knock on her door had been so much better than a buzzing alarm clock. Even though the time was three in the morning, she'd slept soundly for way over eight hours. Ten or eleven at least. The big comfy bed and her full tummy had been just what she needed. The shock had come when she realized that her new job, personal assistant to the Knight brothers, was already in full swing.

She was going to New York with Scott, who had told her that Eric had another TBK meeting he was going to attend. When pressed, Scott had assured her that they were still serious about finding out who had used her computer to get into TBK's network. He wanted her to be patient since it would take some effort and time.

Time? For so long it had ticked painfully for Megan. Since her mother's death, every second piled on more hurt. The one shining spot in all the darkness had been her mother's home, the only real thing in the world that was still hers. The Knight Mansion would've paled most of the homes in Preston Hollow or Highland Park in Dallas. Her house wasn't in either but instead was in a part of the city where average, hardworking families lived, people who might've flown once or twice in their life like her, but never in a private luxury jet like she was now. Still, the little house was one place in the world that held the last happy memories of her mother. Before the cancer. Before her mother's death. Before Kip.

She looked out the window at the clouds zooming by. Her only transportation for so long had been her car, or the DART train when

Granny Gremlin wasn't running.

She'd flown with her mother a year before she died. Her mother's sister was the last family member they shared. Aunt Violet's funeral was simple, with only three people attending—Megan and her mom, and the minister. The legroom on that flight didn't compare to this one.

This almost didn't seem real. But it was real. And so was Scott, sitting directly across from her in the plush leather seat.

"When we land, Megan, I've asked Dylan to take you shopping while I'm in my meeting."

"The guy who put the lock on my door. I remember. Shopping for what?"

"Clothes."

"I'll need to know your sizes." She reached for her purse to get out a pen. "Do you think the O'Learys have a notepad I can borrow on this plane?"

He shrugged and grabbed her hand. The touch made her heart race. "You don't need to write this down, Megan. The clothes aren't for me. They're for you."

She shook her head, not pulling free from his hold. "I'll earn my way."

"I know you will." His endearing smile unhinged Megan and a shiver shot through her.

"Then why are you sending me shopping for clothes?" she heard herself ask irritably. "I told you that I'm not a charity case, Mr. Knight."

Scott seemed to take it all in stride. "Agreed." He squeezed her hand and she thought she would melt right there. "You're quite capable, sweetheart. But you're working for TBK now and you get a wardrobe allowance. Let's drop the 'Mr. Knight,' too. We're way past that, okay?" The last part was less a request and more of an order.

"You're just saying that, Scott." She pulled her hand free of his. "I've never heard of a wardrobe allowance before." But why would she? She'd only worked in clerical jobs in small companies, most with only a single location. TBK had offices all around the country and in Canada. Dallas even had an office.

Maybe he was telling the truth about the allowance.

She looked down at her gray slacks and pink blouse. Other than what she'd worn into the courtroom yesterday, it was the most formal outfit she owned. Pretty sad. She was now working with two young Internet moguls, not in a tiny dentist office. How soon would she be walking into boardrooms with some of the richest people in the world? If today was any clue of what the next three months were going to be like, there was a high probability it would be very soon and often.

She glanced back at Scott with his so-very-kind brown eyes. His stare made her tingly inside.

Maybe he only wanted to give her a new wardrobe and was using the pretense of an allowance from TBK to do it.

"What's the allowance total for staff?" she asked, trying to get to the bottom of it. Pride might've been all she had left, but at least it was something.

"At your current level? Twenty grand."

Her jaw dropped. "Twenty thousand dollars. You've got to be kidding."

He smiled. "Do you need more?"

"Stop teasing me." She thought about asking him who else had such a budget for clothing at his company but didn't. "If you want me to up my apparel for TBK I will, but I won't spend a fraction of that kind of money on clothes for myself."

His tone turned firmer, more like Eric's was all the time. "You accepted our deal, Megan, didn't you?"

She nodded.

"Glad you remembered. You will spend every dollar and you will do that today." He grabbed his wallet from his pocket in his jacket. Pulling out a credit card, he handed it to her. "Use this."

"I've never seen this credit card before. I thought Amex only came in green or gold." That was what she had taken from customers at her many public-facing jobs, besides Visa and MasterCard. "This one is black."

"Yes it is, sweetheart. It's a pretty exclusive card. The good thing with it is the sales folks will be happy to help you. It doesn't have a set limit. Don't you dare look at the tags, okay? Dylan's going with you."

"This is too much, Scott. I'm not Julia Roberts and you're not Richard Gere." She held the card out for him to take, but he only stared at her.

"Megan, I'm not trying to make you uncomfortable, but you have to stop pushing back so hard."

She looked back at the black card. *No limits.* Was this what winners of the Powerball jackpot felt like? Stunned, as she was right now? "I don't know what to say. I'm not good at accepting gifts of any kind."

He left his chair and crouched down in front of her. "Megan, make me happy and let me do this for you."

"I want to but it's hard. I've been on my own for so long." She gazed at Scott and saw more than just a handsome, sexy man. He was kind, honest, and caring. He and Eric had turned her entire life around in a flash. Just a couple of days ago, she was in Dallas with absolutely no hope and no options. Familiar territory. Now she was in a private jet, winging her way to New York with the shopping spree of a lifetime hers for the taking.

His eyes narrowed. "Are you still in love with Kip?"

"No," she blurted. "I thought I was in love with him, but I knew on our wedding night I'd made a mistake. He was a damn liar and a user."

"What did he do to you?" Scott's face darkened with apparent anger. Such rage would've been terrifying had it been pointed her direction, but it wasn't. She found it strangely satisfying that his ferociousness was leveled against Kip for his harm to her, even though she'd yet to tell him what it was.

"He lied to me, Scott. I'd lost my mother to cancer and he came into my life. Flashy and flirty, he swept away my grief." She raised the black Amex card between them for a moment. "He must've had one of these, though I don't remember ever seeing him use it. He always used cash, lots of it."

"Megan, I'm sorry. Did he buy you clothes? Did my offer remind you of him?"

"No, Scott. He never bought me anything, except dinner a few times. He did take me for many rides in his Maserati, though. He wasn't like you and Eric. Very different. He wanted all the limelight and I was happy to let him have it just to keep my sadness and loneliness at bay." The ancient pain welled up inside her like a rising flood. "Why am I telling you this? You don't want to hear my troubles."

Once again, he grabbed not one, but both her hands. "I do, sweetheart. I want to hear it all. Please."

Where Eric's intensity came in shiver-inducing commands, Scott's took the shape of gentle, mouthwatering nudges. Both were impossible to resist.

"I'd only known him for a month when he proposed. God, I was such an idiot. A month?"

"Don't be so hard on yourself. Eric and I fell for Kip's lies, too."

How did Scott know just what to say to make her feel better? She wanted to be touched by him, to be kissed by him, to be held in his arms, exposed. Scott embodied every hero she'd ever read in her erotic romance novels. Sexy. Protective. Dangerous. Kind. A dichotomy of characteristics that appealed to her on every level was right in front of her in flesh and blood, hot male flesh and blood. Her mind might still be resisting, but her body was literally warming to the possibility.

"I guess I shouldn't. My mother's illness took all my focus and hers from my sixteenth birthday until her death four years later and two months before I met the bastard. I graduated high school only because my mother demanded that I did. I felt so lost. I accepted Kip's offer of marriage mainly because I was terrified of being alone again. The very next day we drove to Vegas."

"Kip hated planes. I remember that about him."

"Yes, he did. We stayed at the Monte Carlo. Did you know that in Las Vegas, you can get a marriage license and be married the same day? I didn't. Not back then. Even then, Kip had to ply me with drinks to get me to agree to go through with it."

"Fuck him." Scott growled his disapproval.

Again, his rage made her feel better. She hadn't told anyone this story. Hell, she hadn't had anyone close enough to tell, no family, no friends, no one. Telling Scott felt right. Her heart was already on board, but her mind held back, if only a little.

"I've tried to figure out a way to get a divorce." The word *divorce* was a little off the mark since what she really had been trying to do was get her marriage annulled. Instead of correcting herself, she went on. "I don't have the money and I don't know where the government is keeping him."

"Megan, did he ever touch you?"

She knew that Scott meant physical abuse but the answer was the same, though she decided not to elaborate.

How could she tell him that she was still a virgin? *A twenty-five-year-old virgin.* Most didn't believe such a creature existed, but here she was. Married, too. Impossible.

"No. Kip never touched me."

Chapter Seven

Scott watched Megan's lips quiver. Eric was the one with the sixth sense when it came to women, but he wasn't without his talents. She had told some of the tale of her time with Kip, but she was still holding back. What? He wasn't sure, but he had to find out. Yes, patience with her was required, much patience. After all she'd been through—losing her mother so young, being manipulated by that bastard, having every possession taken from her—she deserved his and Eric's patience and more.

"I'm here for you, sweetheart. No judgment. Talk to me." The one revelation that had come in this flight to New York was he would never let Megan go. Ever.

"I don't want to talk about this anymore." Her hands were trembling and he watched her clasp them together in a clear attempt to steady them.

A whiff of her scent filled his nostrils and his cock stiffened in his pants. But it was more than lust for her that burned through his body. Her trusting him with the details of her past had forever sealed him to her. She was his. Always. He grabbed onto the connection he felt to Megan with his entire being. Yes, he would marry her, but he would never be more committed to Megan than he was right now, here on this plane.

He touched her cheek. "All right, sweetheart."

She grabbed his wrist with her tiny hands, holding his fingers in place on her face. Her sweet, needy sigh thrilled him. It made him feel wanted and powerful.

Megan released his wrist. "Sorry."

"Stop," he said, his Dom skills moving to the forefront and keeping his fingertips on her soft skin. "We have time to enjoy ourselves, sweetheart, before we land."

He wasn't going to fuck her here, on the plane, though the blistering fervor inside him was becoming more difficult to hold back. Making love to her would come in the right way, the only way he knew, with his brother. Sharing Megan with Eric couldn't come any sooner. Scott knew it would be Nirvana.

I've got to get a taste of her sweetness. His cock and balls stood up and saluted that thought.

"What about the pilot?" Her eyes darted to the closed door of the cockpit.

"I agree with you. Need to make sure we have some privacy." Without moving an inch from her, he reached for the intercom and clicked it on.

"Yes, Mr. Knight?" The pilot's voice came through the speaker.

"How long before we touch down?" Watching Megan's sudden quivers mesmerized him.

"Two more hours, sir."

"We're going to get some shut-eye," he informed, loving how cute she looked chewing on her lower lip.

"Very good, sir. I won't disturb you until fifteen minutes before we land."

"Perfect." He clicked off the intercom. "Feel better?"

"Yes, Scott."

"Do you like me touching you?"

She nodded.

"I thought so. I bet you'll like this, too." He leaned down and devoured her mouth with his. The whimper she rewarded his ears inflamed his hunger for more. What started as a gentle touch of her luscious mouth, he willingly intensified into a greedy melding of their lips. He traced her lips with his tongue, loving the taste of honey on them. He demanded entrance into her mouth and she surrendered quickly. The parting of her lips fueled his already burning appetite.

He felt her hands wrap around his neck, her fingers locking together. Plunging his tongue into her delicious mouth, he pulled Megan into his body until he could feel more of her soft flesh. He released her mouth, moving to her neck. She was so tiny and vulnerable, and his crushing need to possess and protect blasted through him and down into his cock and balls.

He wanted her, wanted all of her. He swept her up in his arms and sat back down in his seat, pulling her down on him. The feel of her round bottom on his cock, even with their clothing creating a thin barrier of fabric, made his pulse pound hard and hot in his veins. He kissed her again—a wordless claim but a claim indeed. She was his. She would be Eric's, too. His cock was responding to the wiggle of her bottom full on, lengthening to the near-painful.

Two hours was not enough time for all he wanted to do to her. But there *was* enough to get her hot and bothered, screaming for more. He would pleasure her until she couldn't imagine ever being without him. Once he and Eric could get her into the playroom between them, she would be theirs forever.

His cravings thundered hard, but he forced himself to relax. She deserved him to be a lover, not an animal. But fuck, he felt like an animal now, with Megan's fingers playing in his hair, their tongues melding together in her mouth, and his cock throbbing to the brink of painful.

He twisted her blonde locks between his fingers and gave them the slightest tug. Her eyes fluttered and her lips vibrated as he continued kissing her. The little mewl that came from her throat shot up his desire to claim her. As he moved his left hand to the nape of her neck and his right hand to her shoulder, he realized how overwhelming his need for Megan had become in only two days. Absurd to most, but absolutely and utterly true to him.

He released her lips and gazed into her green blinking eyes.

Her cute nose wrinkled. "Why are you and Eric helping me?"

He cupped her chin. "Because you need us and we can."

And again, he crushed his mouth to hers. Kissing had never been his thing before. It had always been a means to a desired finish line. But with Megan, kissing was so much more and so very necessary. His heart thudded in his chest and his blood seared through his veins and down to his cock. Her lips were soft and inviting. Everything about her was soft, inviting, and so much more. She was his world. He would do anything he had to do to win her and to make her happy.

Ending their kiss, he closed his hands over Megan's voluptuous breasts.

"Are you sure we should do this?" she asked meekly.

"What? You don't like kissing, baby?" He leaned forward and gently merged their lips together once again.

Tenderly he massaged her breasts. Her tiny hot pants into his mouth made him even harder, hungrier, and wild with heavy need. He let go of her lips and her mouth dropped open.

Her cheeks were bright red and her pupils were dilated. "Scott, I–I adore kissing you, but—"

"Shh. Let's just enjoy ourselves and see where this goes. I'll take this only as far as you want. Not one inch farther. Okay?"

"Yes." She nodded so sweetly. "I'm very inexperienced when it comes to this kind of thing."

Every breath and syllable made her chest shiver in his hands. He had to control himself. Keep his head. He must. "Sweetheart, I've got the reins here. Understand?"

She sighed and then smiled, inflaming him beyond reason. Then she surprised him with what she asked next. "Will you tell me about that room at your mansion with the bench-looking thing? You know, the room where Eric shut the door when I first arrived."

"What do you want to know about the playroom?" Scott knew it would've been best if Eric were with them right now instead of in Dallas. From the very beginning, their sexual experiences were mainly together. Sure, they'd each had a few tumbles alone, but they both preferred to share a woman's bed most of the time. When they'd become official instructors at Phase Four, that choice was advanced in them even more. In Destiny, poly relationships were quite normal and even expected.

"I've read some books about people into that kind of lifestyle. Are you and Eric...well, are you?"

"You mean BDSM?"

"Yes." Her tone was tiny and feminine, her scent intoxicating and full of need. "Bondage and dominance is what I am curious about. Is that what you and your brother built the room for?"

His blood pulsed into his cock until the pressure felt unbearable. He inhaled deeply, capturing every wisp of her that floated in the air of the plane. His mouth watered. He couldn't wait to get his tongue on her sweet pussy.

"We're men of many tastes, Megan." He lightly caressed her gorgeous tits. "How about you? What do you like?"

She shrugged. "I really don't know. Like I said, I'm not that experienced."

He sensed there was more to that than she was willing to say. As much as he wanted to press her to trust him, he didn't. In the library and down in the shooting range, he and Eric had talked about being patient with her. He could hit the accelerator to the floorboard and steamroll her into surrendering all to him, but what then? She would bolt as soon as she could. She was curious but also nervous, even scared. So instead of pressing for the truth, he found her taut nipples under her blouse with his thumb and forefinger.

He pinched her fleshy tips ever so lightly, then asked, "What does this feel like?"

She tilted her head back slightly and her lips began to quiver. "Nice."

He kept himself in check by sheer willpower. His inner caveman wanted to claim her for his own right then and there.

"Close your eyes, Megan."

She instantly obeyed and his lust doubled and tripled. It was clear to him that Megan was curious to dip her toe into the sexual waters of BDSM but was hesitant about it. God, training and teaching her all that BDSM had to offer would be the greatest pleasure of his life. But now he could only imply what the Dom/sub relationship consisted of. Later, with Eric's help, the lessons could go deep, really deep.

"Inside your body, what are you feeling? Tell me," he instructed.

"Hot tingly things." She opened her eyes and looked him square in the face, her hand skimming his cheek. "It feels wonderful, Scott. I know about how things work in your hometown, in your mansion." She blinked and then looked down at her feet so cutely.

He continued to knead her breasts and pinch her nipples. "If you're asking if we have shared women, the answer is 'yes.'"

Trembling, she returned her gaze back to him. "Phoebe told me about the O'Learys, Judge Ethel and her two husbands. I've never heard of such a thing before."

"Don't knock it until you've tried it, sweetheart." Scott wanted to fuel her curiosity but also to quell her concerns. "But I don't want to talk about our pasts, do you? I would much rather talk about right now. You and me. Here on this plane. Together." With the skill of a well-trained Dom, he'd already determined her bra's clasp was in the front. Keeping his left hand on her breasts, he brushed the skin of her neck with his tongue. With his right hand, he reached under her blouse and unfastened her bra, giving his fingertips a fabric-free access to her incredible tits.

Her breathing became shallow.

"I've got to see your beauties, baby. Time for the big reveal."

Her sweet, nervous laugh thrilled him. "Am I supposed to call you 'Sir' now?"

Fuck yeah, you should.

Her question shot straight into his cock. "I know you've read some about the life, but reading is different than doing. I've got the reins, sweetheart. We're just having fun. This isn't a scene or play.

You haven't been trained. You don't know the protocols."

She smiled. "One day I would like to ask you more about it, if you don't mind, Scott?" Delicious-looking gooseflesh popped up on her arms, and her face and neck turned the cutest shade of red, delighting his eyes.

"It would be my pleasure." His heart was leaping for joy. Megan was the perfect woman for him, for Eric. She was interested in the life, and that galvanized him through and through.

What more could he ask for? When her eyes had widened at the sight of the mansion's playroom, he'd longed—but held little faith—for a day when she would consider visiting it again. Now, hope swelled in his chest, becoming something powerful and certain. She would not only visit the dungeon, she would enjoy it with him and Eric.

Continuing to caress her breast with his right hand, he used his left to brush her silky hair out of her eyes. "You're enjoying this, but I sense you're a little anxious, right?"

Chapter Eight

Megan gazed into Scott's brown eyes. "I am a little nervous. Like I told you, I'm not very skilled in the bedroom."

It was wrong, she knew it was wrong, but she couldn't seem to bring herself to tell him the truth—that she was a virgin, that the extent of her sexual exposure came from books.

Until now, on this plane with Scott, kissing had been the pinnacle of intimacy for her. She'd dreamed about this moment, the moment a man would take her virginity. But being with Scott was much more than any of those nighttime fantasies. This was tactile, intense, bright, and so very real. Scott was like the heroes of her favorite books— protective, loyal, relentless, and mouthwatering, panty-drenching sexy.

But this was wrong. He should know, shouldn't he? It wasn't right to keep such a thing from him. And she was married. Sure, she didn't want to be, but legally, she still was.

She was about to open her mouth and tell him everything when he spoke. "I've waited long enough. I've got to see your tits, Megan."

Her head reeled as Scott removed her top over her head. Her trembles intensified to major quakes. Words wouldn't come. Not yet. She wanted to feel his fingertips on her skin, his lips on her mouth. If she told him now, would he be shocked? Would he stop? She couldn't bear the thought. She'd never felt her body get so warm before. Moisture pooled between her legs. She would tell him the truth before they took the final plunge. He was due that from her. But for now, right or wrong, she would ride the wave of his masculinity. She wanted more, needed more, craved more.

He pulled her already unfastened bra apart, exposing every inch of her chest. She'd always felt her breasts were too big for her body, but the way he was looking at them, Megan thought she might've be wrong.

"Gorgeous. My God, you have the most beautiful tits I've ever seen, sweetheart." Without a word, his mouth came down on her right nipple, sending a shock through her body and a gasp out of her mouth.

His thick, manly lips tightened around the tip of her nipple, delivering a sweet sting that reached all the way down into her pussy. Her clit began to throb.

Scott wanted her. Really wanted her.

Through every fiber of her being, she wanted him, too. She stretched out her hand tentatively, still not quite sure what was typical with this level of intimacy, but she had to touch his ruggedly handsome face. When he nodded his approval, she moved her fingertips to his square jaw. His five-o'clock shadow brushed her flesh, delivering a quick shock that traveled up her arm, down her torso, and parked itself in her clit, pulsating to the very edge of where logic and sanity bordered frenzy and delirium. Cravings that she'd never experienced before rolled through, sweeping away her resistance. She wondered what lay beneath Scott's shirt, his jeans. He might run circles around a boardroom, but he looked like a man more comfortable in a saddle than in an executive's chair.

"You want to see my chest, don't you?"

Like a mentalist, Scott could apparently see into her very thoughts. "Yes. Very much."

"Fair is fair." He cupped her breasts in his giant hands and sent her a wicked wink. Then he shed his clothes slowly, certainly for her benefit. She was finding it hard to swallow when he tossed his shirt to the plane's floor. A sun-soaked, muscled chest and ripped abdomen came into view. "Touch me."

She obeyed him, running her fingers over his hard flesh.

"Now we're both bare-chested. Better?"

"Much," she answered, continuing to caress his upper half's perfection.

His hands moved down her sides. She loved the feel of his rough fingers on her body. Wherever he touched her, new sensations she'd never felt before sprung up. The man definitely knew his way around a woman's body, which was quite rewarding to her.

In a flash, he lifted her up in his arms. She wrapped her legs around his waist and her arms around his shoulders, balancing herself in his hold.

"I don't know about you, baby, but I want to see more of you. Would you like to see more of me?"

She most definitely did. "Yes. Please. Fair is fair." She repeated his words.

"There's a sweet, little vixen inside you, isn't there, sweetheart?"

She took a deep breath, uncertainty crushing back in. Closing her eyes, she tried to steady herself. *Vixen wannabe? Maybe, but definitely not a full-fledged vixen.*

"Megan, what's the matter?" he asked, lowering her to her previous seat.

"I want to do this right, Scott. I want you to be happy with my performance."

His eyebrows shot up. "Darling, you don't have to perform anything. I guess it has been a long time since you've done this. I told you before, I'm in control, I'm responsible here, not you. Your job is to open yourself up and feel." He cradled her chin in his hand. "You think you can do that for me?"

Tears welled in her eyes. "Yes."

As his fingertips touched her cheek, she was engulfed in the potency of this moment. Scott was everything she'd ever dreamed of—gentle when she needed him to be, demanding other times, for just the same reason.

He knelt in front of her, his hands on the top of her thighs and his stare intense and locked on her eyes.

It was time to tell him the truth, but once again, before she could, his passionate moves muted her. The latest was the removal of the rest of her clothing, including her panties, which were now the only thing on her, though at her ankles instead of covering her pussy.

Forcing her eyes to remain open, she glanced at the man mere inches from her most intimate flesh.

"That's the most beautiful thing I've ever seen." His awestruck words seemed genuine to her. He leaned down, moving his face closer, closer, closer until she could feel his hot, manly breath skate across her damp mound and blast into her clit. Violent tension welled up inside her until she had to bite her lip and grip the armrests of her chair to keep from screaming.

"God, you smell so good," he said and then painted her abdomen with kisses.

Here. There. Everywhere.

A new bout of shivers, more intense and powerful than any of the earlier ones, rolled through her as his thick, manly lips continued working her over but never moving lower, where she needed them most. He squeezed her thighs, and crazed urges took hold of all of her. She tried to widen her legs in an attempt to invite him down, but he held her in place.

"No you don't, baby. I'm running this show."

She was unable to hold back any longer. "Please, Scott. I can't take much more."

"Since you said 'please,' I think you've earned your reward." Scott removed her panties. Then he lifted her legs until they were over his shoulders and his head was settled right between them. When his tongue traced through her folds, new moisture saturated her pussy.

More kisses landed on her. One after another. When she felt Scott's thumb on her clit, she nearly came out of her seat. When he pressed the sensitive bundle of nerves, her hands, which had been clutching the armrests, shot up to his shoulders and neck. Mad with passion, she spread her legs even wider, wanting to feel everything

Scott had to offer. Everything.

Over and over he licked and sucked and pressed her sex, raising her temperature, her hunger, her need for release. She trusted him to get her there.

When he pushed a finger into her pussy while capturing her clit with his lips, Megan thought she might actually pass out. Every inch of her body was vibrating with sensations. This was an orgasm—a real, bona fide, undeniable, overwhelming orgasm.

Scott continued lapping up her juices, and then he sent another finger deep into her pussy, which clenched hard around them, adding to the ride of release. She squeezed Scott's head with her thighs, pressing them together like a vise. She never wanted this to end, Scott's mouth and fingers working over her sex in ways she'd never imagined.

She was finding it hard to breathe into the explosive pleasure detonating inside her.

"Drown me, baby. I want all your sweet cream."

His lusty words added to the inferno she was feeling. It went on and on. In her current state of release, she had no sense of time or space. She floated in a warm space in her mind. Satiated, her trembles began to back down slightly.

If this was what oral sex was like, she couldn't even imagine what intercourse would be. She was ready, ready to be taken, to give to Scott something she would never be able to give again.

Abruptly the plane shook, startling her. Scott leaned back but kept his hands on her thighs.

The pilot's voice came over the speakers. "Sorry about that. It's going to be bumpy the rest of the way. I'd recommend you fasten your seat belts."

Scott smiled at her. He stood up, allowing her a perfect view of him. The outline of his massive cock was clearly visible in his jeans. She gulped at the size of the thing.

He clicked the intercom. "Thanks, Colton." His naked chest

glistened as he grabbed her top. "You enjoyed yourself?"

"Yes," she said, suddenly nervous again. She enveloped her chest with her arms and lessened the view of her pussy as much as she could by squeezing her legs together. Her panties were at her feet and would've been better at covering her pussy, but she didn't have the courage to reach down and pull them on—not with Scott's hot stare on her.

She lowered her eyes to her knees, feeling the shivers again in her body.

"Look at me, Megan."

Trembling, she lifted her gaze back to him.

"My God, you are so beautiful." He leaned down and melded their mouths together once again. She felt one of his hands on the back of her head and the other on the curve in her waist, both pulling her closer into him.

Instinctively, she moved her arms off her breasts and to Scott. As her fingertips touched his hard flesh and he deepened his kiss, her heart surrendered to the man who had given her pleasure—her first sexual experience beyond masturbation. They might not have gone all the way, but it was farther down the road then she'd ever been, that was for sure.

Another shake of the plane, and he ended their kiss. "We better get in our seats, baby." He knelt down and grabbed her panties. In a flash, he helped her on with them and the rest of her clothes.

He buckled her in, and then he put his shirt back on.

She'd been about to tell him the truth when the turbulence hit.

"You okay, Megan?" Scott asked so respectfully.

"Yes. Thank you." She could tell him right now about her virginity. *Right now.* He opened his laptop up and began typing away, preparing for his meeting. "Scott?"

He looked up from the screen. "What is it?"

Right now?

She would tell him everything but not now. She just couldn't. "Is there something I could be working on for you? I am your personal assistant, aren't I?"

"Actually, I'm going to need your help on a charity event that Eric and I are sponsoring. It's a citywide paintball game..."

As Scott clued her in on Destiny's Annual Paintball Extravaganza, her insides tingled nice and warm.

She would wait for the perfect time to tell him. That just wasn't right now.

Chapter Nine

Eric watched Josh pick the lock on Megan's house.

Josh was the son of Takahiro, who preferred to be called "Hiro," and Melissa Phong, the owners of the Chinese restaurant in Destiny. Eric and Scott had known Josh since elementary school. He favored his mother's Italian heritage more than his father's Japanese, though his eyes appeared more Asian.

This Dallas neighborhood was circa 1940s. Under a thousand square feet was apparently the norm here. Most of the homes were pretty dicey, and a few were even boarded up. Megan's wasn't the worst of the lot, but only by a little. Three of her windows didn't have screens. The paint was peeling off.

His gut tightened at the thought of her living in this dilapidated area.

If Josh couldn't pick the lock and get the door open, it wouldn't stop Eric from going inside and getting her modem. The door was hollow-core, which wasn't meant for exteriors let alone to act as a front door. Breaking it down would be easy and might help tamp down his frustration, like thirty minutes punching a bag at Destiny's Boxing Gym did most of the time. Megan was in real danger, and he needed to know who was behind it all so that he could direct his anger to the guilty person.

"Almost got it." Josh continued working on the lock.

Eric looked up and down the street. No sign of anyone, but he was certain they were being watched from behind some windows. Would any of them call the police? Maybe. He didn't care. They wouldn't be here long enough for that to matter. In and out. Get the modem and be gone.

Josh stood up and pushed the door open. "After you."

"What other skills do you have that I should be worried about?"

Josh smiled. "More than I can count."

Eric walked in and stopped in his tracks. This was *her* home. *Hers.* Megan's. Kip had lived here with her for a few weeks. He clenched his jaw at the thought.

"You okay, buddy?" Josh said quietly, placing a hand on his shoulder.

"I'm fine." But he wasn't. Just in the front door in a tiny entry area, he could see the place was neat, as he expected it would be. Megan was that kind of woman. But neatness didn't change the fact that living here must've been hard for her these past five years.

The floors were pine and in really bad condition. Two poor patch jobs took up half the entry's boards. To his right was a utility room with washer and dryer hookups but no washer or dryer. To his left was a very short hallway—smaller than the tiniest of closets in his home in Destiny. The passage led to three doors that were all hanging open, revealing a bathroom through one, an empty room that was likely meant to be a bedroom through another, and through the last door, he saw a futon.

Megan's room, the place she slept.

His pulse pounded in his temples and his heart ached for her and the suffering she'd endured. If he and Scott hadn't left Kip to run the Dallas office, she would've never met him, never been brought so low.

Instead of going down the hall to those rooms, Eric moved forward into the living room. It was narrow, only eleven feet wide but twenty feet long. It had to be the biggest room in the tiny house. The only furniture here was a card table with four metal chairs. Three boxes, one with books inside and the other two empty, sat in the corner. An ancient-looking television that looked more like a box than a set was on top of a plastic crate. Next to it was the modem he'd come to Dallas to retrieve.

"Was she robbed?" Josh asked, clearly confused by the lack of items here.

"Only by her fucking husband and his crimes." This might've been a beautiful home at one time but it wasn't now. It didn't have even the simplest of bare necessities. "Let's get what we came for and get out of here."

She was never coming back here. He would see to that. He would make sure whoever had piggybacked on her IP to hack TBK's systems would be found and brought down. He would make sure she was safe, and he could see himself doing that for the rest of his life.

"Should we see if there are some personal items Megan wants us to bring back?" Josh asked.

"That's why I brought you here with me," Eric said. "You know me. I'm a nuts-and-bolts guy. Sentiment is often lost on me."

"That, and you trust me to keep my mouth shut."

Eric nodded. "True. Don't disappoint me."

Josh smiled. "I never have."

He pulled out his cell but remembered she and Scott were still in the air. They wouldn't be landing for another hour. "You know what? Instead of picking and choosing, let's take everything back with us." He grabbed one of the empty boxes.

"Shouldn't be a problem. I'll load up the stuff in here." Josh lifted up the television. "You should be the one to check her closet and bathroom."

He'd told Josh about the reason they were going to Megan's house, but he hadn't mentioned how he felt about her. But the guy was one of the few people who could read him. Scott was one of the most intuitive Doms at Phase Four, but Josh held the crown for being able to get into almost anyone's head.

"Deal." Eric walked into her bedroom first.

He leaned down and touched the black pad of the futon. Her scent, though faint, was still in the room. His dick hardened. The green-eyed beauty was in his every thought and the reason for his current actions. Never had he been so locked into one woman before, but he knew whatever he had to do to keep her safe, to keep her happy, to keep her with him, he would do. He'd quench hell's fires and tear down heaven's gates if he had to. Whatever it took, he would succeed at winning her heart.

He opened her closet door, and once again a pang of sadness for Megan washed over him. Two pairs of jeans hung on wire hangers— one so threadbare it should have been tossed long ago and the other close behind its sibling. Five cotton tops also hung in the closet. On the single shelf above were some bras and panties, neatly folded and stacked. If he had any say in things, and he meant to have more than a say, Megan wouldn't need undergarments, especially when they were alone.

Eric started placing Megan's clothes in the box he'd grabbed from the living room when his cell rang. He looked at the screen and saw Vicky Bates's name and office number.

"Fuck."

* * * *

Megan looked at the intimidating building.

She and Dylan were standing in front of Bergdorf Goodman. Men and women wearing the most modern and sophisticated clothes she'd ever seen walked by them into the department store.

She didn't belong inside. Her outfit made her feel conspicuous, and not in the good way. "I can't go in there. They won't give me the time of day."

"I have strict instructions, Mrs. Lunceford." Scott had sent Dylan with her on this shopping event while he attended his meeting.

Dylan, with his dark suit and shades, looked more befitting to protect the president than someone like her, but Scott had insisted. Never having been in New York before, she'd reluctantly agreed.

Luckily only a few people gawked at them, and according to Dylan, they were likely tourists not locals.

"Surely there's a Target or Walmart we can find while Scott's in his meeting."

Dylan's manner was of a man on constant guard, surveying every nook and cranny, every passerby, every detail. Even so, there was an ease she sensed about him, under all the military training he'd most certainly been through. He'd likely seen action.

"The schedule is clear. First here. We ask for Nina. She's got everything set up for you to try on. The Louis Vuitton store is next. Michelle is there." He glanced at his cell and then at her. "Tiffany's. Frank. Piaget. Kevin. Prada. Beth. Then we head up Fifth to the Hermès shop. Klaussen will be outfitting you with a particular handbag that Scott has chosen for you. Last, we backtrack to the Apple store. Our point man is Terry. There we will secure your MacBook Pro, iPad, and iPhone. That's where we rendezvous with Scott."

Dylan had a strange way of making a shopping spree sound like a covert operation. "That's quite a list, but I guess men in black are used to lists. You're the one who tracked down the hacker to my house, aren't you?"

He nodded, motioning to the door of their first stop. "Shall we?"

"In a minute." She had to know what he thought about her now. "Tell me, Dylan, do you believe I'm guilty."

He lowered his arm. "Does it matter either way?"

"Maybe it shouldn't but it does to me. Scott and Eric apparently trust you." Her voice shook in her throat as her feelings for the Knights bubbled up to the forefront. "Please. It may be silly to someone like you, but it isn't to me."

He removed his glasses, which surprised her. His eyes narrowed and he didn't say a word for several seconds, making her wish she could take back the question.

Finally, he said, "The only time we've seen each other was in the courtroom, at the mansion, and most recently in the limo ride from TBK's office downtown to Fifth Avenue. That's not a long time to determine such a thing for an investigator."

She sighed. "I thought so."

"But I'm not an average investigator, Megan. I'm the best. You're innocent. I know it."

Thrilled with his words, she hugged him. "Thank you. Thank you."

"You're welcome. Now, I have a job to do and you're keeping me from it."

"Right. Sorry." She released him.

He put his aviators back on. "After you, Mrs. Lunceford."

Chapter Ten

Eric stared at the two words below Vicky's name and number. The green one was *answer* and the red one was *decline*. Thinking it better to take the call than to put her off, he placed the box on Megan's futon and clicked the green word.

"Hey, Vicky."

"It's Vicky and Felix," she said. "Got you on speaker."

"Hey, Felix."

Felix voiced, "I thought you guys were going to be in New York talking to Senator Brickman and General Furnish about the delay. What are you doing in Dallas?"

Fuck. "Scott's the lead in New York. I'm here on another matter." He kept his tone level. "How did you know I was in Dallas, anyway? I didn't decide to come here until late last night."

"Trying to pull an unannounced inspection on us, Eric?" Vicky laughed. "Some things never change."

Felix chimed in. "I called the Destiny offices first thing this morning to try to catch you guys before you took off. So I called the airport in Walden. The man there said the flight plan filed had changed from New York to Dallas."

"Eric." Vicky's serious tone made him clench his jaw. "We had another attack into the system."

"When?"

"Last night, five minutes after midnight. That's why you're here, right?" she asked. "You're getting closer to finding the hacker. Is the culprit in Texas?"

Now he and Scott had proof positive that Megan was innocent, like they expected her to be. "Still working on that, Vicky. Not any closer than we were before." Eric didn't want to tip his hand. He would've liked to trust Vicky, but he still wasn't ready to trust anyone besides Scott. He would wait to fill her in only after everything came to light and Megan was safe.

"When can we expect you in the Dallas office, buddy?" Felix asked.

"You can't. I'll be heading back to Destiny today."

"Why so cloak-and-dagger?" TBK's number two in Dallas asked.

Vicky added, "Are you working on a new deal we should know about?"

After seeing Megan's home, the only deal he wanted to work on was keeping her safe, getting to know her better, and ultimately winning her heart.

"Shoot me the details you've got on this last attack. When I get to the office tomorrow, I'll call you so you can fill me in."

"You're the boss," she said with a hint of irritation.

Vicky was ambitious, but was she too ambitious, like Kip had been?

* * * *

Megan walked into the mansion with her arms loaded with packages. It was after midnight, and even though she'd slept nearly the entire flight from New York back to Colorado, she was exhausted.

Scott was beside her with even more packages, and there were still more in his truck.

She shook her head. "I can't keep all of this. It's too much."

"Not this again, sweetheart."

"Scott, you told me that twenty thousand dollars was my TBK wardrobe allowance. We brought back at least double that amount. I'm going to return most of it."

"Megan, please stop," he said, dropping the bags to the floor.

She really didn't know the total since Dylan had taken over paying the bills during the shopping spree. He'd also, per Scott's instructions, kept the salesclerks from telling her how much things cost. But after spying a couple of forgotten tags when they boarded the plane, she knew the budget must've been busted. The Manolo suede boots were nearly fourteen hundred dollars alone.

"This bag"—she patted the camel-colored Hermès—"might be as much as five thousand all by itself."

"More like thirty-five to forty," Eric said, coming down the stairs with Gretchen.

"What?" Her jaw dropped. "How would you know that?"

He shrugged.

"When did you get back?" Scott asked.

"To Destiny? An hour ago. Went to the tower first before coming home. Got here about ten minutes ago."

Gretchen came up to her side and took the shopping bags Megan was holding from her. "Don't let Eric fool you, Megan. As you can tell by his current attire, he's no fashion follower."

"What's wrong with jeans, boots, and T-shirts?" he asked.

"See what I mean? Those and a Stetson, and he's ready to face the day. But I do know how he knows about the price of this magnificent bag." Gretchen grinned. "When these two joined the billionaire club, the designers came out of the woodwork. We get invitations by the truckloads for them. Starlets, too, come sniffing after these lads. What was the one's name who was nominated for an Oscar but lost?"

Eric rolled his eyes. "I went with that actress because TBK was doing business with her uncle's company. It was just business. God, if you bring that up again I won't be responsible for what I do."

Gretchen held up her fists and smiled. "Bring it on, Eric. I'm a card-carrying matriarch of *Fight Club*," she said with a wink. "Oops. I've said too much."

Eric hugged and lifted Gretchen off the floor.

She laughed. "Put me down. I have work to do."

He did and then kissed her on the forehead.

Megan liked how Eric was around Gretchen. It was a side of him she wanted to get to know more. There was real affection between the Knights and the dear lady.

"This handbag is really that much?" Megan asked.

Gretchen walked up to her. "My dear, it doesn't matter. It's a gift."

"But it isn't. It's part of my wardrobe allowance from TBK."

The woman brushed the hair out of her eyes. "Megan, we both know better. The thing you've got to learn is how to accept gifts. I know that must be hard for you. I come from the East End. It's the part of London where families struggle just to get by. My mother and father worked in the garment industry. The only gifts I ever got were an apple on my birthday and another on Christmas in my stocking."

Scott put his arm around Gretchen, but didn't say a word as she continued recounting her upbringing.

"Women like us have trouble accepting gifts. We always think there's some nefarious motive. You've worked hard your whole life, haven't you, dear? You've also known suffering and loss. I can see it in your eyes."

Megan looked at the kind woman and saw a kindred spirit. "I know what you're trying to do. But seriously, this purse is too much." She pointed to the shopping bags on the floor. "These are too much and there are more in the truck. Eric and Scott have been kind and generous. They dropped the lawsuit. That would've been enough."

Scott said, "Megan—"

"Quiet," Gretchen said, cutting him off. "Let her finish and then I will speak. You two can say your piece after, if you have something to say, but not before. Go on, child."

"They offered me a job. That would've been enough. But believing someone had used my computer without my knowledge at my home, they gave me a room here in this palace and a bodyguard. They flew me to New York on a private jet. That would've been enough. But this?" Again, she motioned to the piles of purchases. "It's too much. I can't accept it."

"Your pride is getting in the way of you really seeing this for what it is, Megan," Gretchen said. "I've been with these boys for many years. Their parents were still alive, God rest their souls." The woman did the sign of the cross over her chest. "Rich people in their own right. Eric and Scott were so young when they lost them, not even out of high school yet. I tried to console them the best I could but their grief was more than even I could help with. Luckily, the O'Learys stepped in. For Irish folks, they aren't half bad. Being English myself, not a big fan of the Emerald Isle." She winked, clearly trying to lighten the mood. "Patrick and Sam took these two, the Stone boys, and the three Coleman children under their wings. With their help, Eric and Scott found a way to channel their sadness into another outlet, making money, and the money they made kept multiplying their inheritance again and again. And you know where they stand now. Billionaires."

"I'm not sure what this has to do with me, Gretchen, or all this merchandise I need to return."

"Listen to yourself, Megan. Of course you're uncomfortable. It's a lot to take in. Eric and Scott have never been slow to boil."

Megan absolutely had experienced that.

"These and all the rest." Gretchen picked up several of the shopping bags. "Can't you see this is my boys' way of trying to win your heart?"

She'd come to expect bad things—abandonment, betrayal, heartache. That worldview resided deep inside every fiber of Megan's being. Since Kip, keeping her guard up was as natural to her as breathing. No one would ever want her, not really, not forever. What did she have to offer anyone? Nothing. And men like Scott and Eric, who had everything? Again, nothing. But what if Gretchen was right? What if they were trying to win her heart?

"Gifts aside, there's more to Eric and Scott than just stubbornness and bravado." Gretchen kissed her on the cheek. "Take the leap of faith. You know you want to. Open yourself up, Megan, and you'll see."

She sucked in a deep breath and glanced at Scott and Eric. They were giving the one-two punch to her resolve and Gretchen was about to land a knockout. "Does this dear woman always play matchmaker for you two?"

Scott shook his head. "We found you before Gretchen ever met you, sweetheart. She's a hopeless romantic, yes?" He kissed Gretchen on the top of her head.

"My turn," Eric said. "Megan needs her rest. It's been a very long day."

His words seemed to reach into her, and her tired and tensed muscles relaxed, as she imagined how good it would feel to get into her big, comfy bed.

"For all of you," Gretchen added. "There's some stew in the kitchen I've kept warm for you. Go. I'll put away your things. Your beds are all turned down and ready for you when you finish your meal."

Megan walked between the Knight brothers, still holding the Hermès bag and thinking about what Gretchen had said.

She inhaled the aroma of Gretchen's stew before they even got to the kitchen, one of the many spaces in the mansion she hadn't seen yet. The room was decked with every appliance and contraption that would've left even world-class chefs drooling. The attention to detail in every single inch of the kitchen was easy to see. Copper pots of every shape and size hung above the eight-burner range in the center of the massive granite island.

Eric pulled out a chair for her at the long counter. "Have a seat, Megan."

The butterflies in her stomach just wouldn't settle, not after Gretchen's revelation in the foyer. "Thank you," she said, sitting down. She blew out a breath to try to calm her nerves. No help.

Scott went to the cabinet and pulled out three bowls. Eric got some spoons for them out of one of the kitchen drawers. Being waited on was still new to her but she definitely liked it.

"What would you like to drink, sweetheart?" Scott asked.

"Water is fine."

Scott turned to Eric. "How about you?"

"Same for me." Eric began loading up their bowls with Gretchen's savory-smelling stew. "Here you go." He pushed the first bowl in front of her.

She leaned down and inhaled the medley. It smelled yummy, and her stomach grumbled again, reminding her it had been nearly seven hours since her last meal that consisted of a salad and a Coke Zero.

Eric placed a bowl on each side of her, clearly meaning to hem her in between his brother and him. He took the seat to her left and Scott the one to her right.

"Dig in, baby." Scott didn't wait for her to start eating. He dove right in, clearly enjoying his meal.

She'd never seen anyone eat so fast. Dylan had insisted on breaking up her shopping trip, getting her a salad before they went to the Hermès store. But when had Scott had time to eat? The answer was that he hadn't.

She lowered her spoon into the thick broth. Before she could bring it up to her mouth, she noticed Eric hadn't made a single move to eat any of his stew. Instead, his eyes were fixed on her like a smoking-hot laser, heating her insides and making her fidgety.

"Aren't you going to eat?" she asked him, feeling a shiver run up her spine and down again.

He nodded. "After you, Megan."

Gretchen's words echoed through her again and again. *Can't you see this is my boys' way of trying to win your heart?*

What if she let her walls down with Eric and Scott? What then? Destiny wasn't like Dallas or any other place on the planet, she would bet. Marriages consisted of multiples here, and the Knight brothers were no exception. She couldn't deny she was attracted to both of them. Charming. Handsome. Generous.

They were the type of men any woman would be thrilled to share her bed with. But both? Her books painted worlds where such a thing was possible.

But this is real life.

She was flesh and blood, not some creation from the mind of a writer. Whatever happened here, life would go on. She'd wanted to crawl under a rock and die after Kip's arrest and losing everything. But she hadn't. She'd had to pick up the pieces and work through it. That was how things went.

"Why aren't you eating, Megan?" Eric's blue-eyed stare burned into her. She trembled.

"Not hungry, I guess."

Scott put down his spoon. His bowl was completely empty. "That can't be true. Dylan told me what you had to eat. A salad. You must be famished."

"She is. She's lying." Eric's eyes narrowed and his face darkened.

She gulped. "Okay. I'm thinking about what Gretchen said in the foyer."

"Better," he said. "Continue."

There were differences between the two that gave her pause.

Scott was open. After their plane ride to New York, she couldn't stop thinking how incredible it would be to have his lips again, kissing her body everywhere.

Eric wasn't so open. What was underneath all that dark danger and sexiness? Did she really want to know? God help her, she did. Eric had a tender side with Gretchen, but would he with anyone else? Would he with her?

"Megan, I'm waiting," Eric said.

Scott was patient. Eric was clearly not.

"I'm not sure what to think or say about all this. Phoebe filled me in on how things work around here. *Poly* is the term, right?"

"It is. And…?"

What she'd felt coming from Eric and Scott completely unhinged her. They were like two sides of the same coin. Together they created a single steamy blend that awakened something new inside her, something she couldn't control.

"I'm not sure that's something I can do." Why had she said that? Because it was true. Now would be a good time to tell them she was a virgin. *Now. Say it, Megan.* But the words wouldn't come. What would they think of her once they knew the truth?

"Why?" Eric said, grabbing her hand and squeezing.

She looked into his eyes and saw something unexpected directed her way. Tenderness and concern. "I'm scared."

"You would be stupid not to be, and I know you're not stupid. You made it on your own after the Kip debacle. That's quite an achievement."

Now. Tell him the part of the "Kip debacle" they didn't know. "I didn't really do too well with that."

Eric put his index finger to her lips. "Let me finish. Being frightened is very appropriate, Megan. It's how the human species has survived so long. Knowing when to fight and when to hide is critical to making it to the next day. You've done that and more. Scott told me about you wanting to divorce Kip but that you couldn't get through all the government bureaucracy. What did you do? You put that away for another day and worked on what was right in front of you so that you could survive."

She looked at him in stunned silence.

He cupped her chin. "When are you going to stop beating yourself up, Megan?"

"I don't know if I can. It's been so hard," she confessed. "I've done my best but it's never been enough." Ancient tears welled up in her eyes.

"You're kidding, right?" Scott stroked her hair. "Anyone else would've gone over the deep end, but not you. You're a fighter. You get knocked down and you get right back up."

Looking from one to the other, she began to tremble. Two men, so different in personality, brothers, wanted her, wanted to share her, wanted to win her. The truth was they'd already captured her heart. In their eyes, she saw a future that she'd never even dreamed of.

"Enough," Eric stated firmly. "Words can only convince her so far."

While Scott rubbed her neck with his massive hands, Eric leaned over and pressed his thick, manly lips to her mouth. Her insides exploded with wicked shivers. His toe-curling kiss went on and on.

When Eric finally released her lips, her pussy was soaked. His eyes raked over her, assessing and shameless.

Scott's fingertips skated along the back of her arms.

A dangerous smile spread over Eric's face, one dark brow going up. "Are you ready to take the leap of faith, little one?"

Little one. It was the first time he'd called her anything other than her name. She squeezed her thighs together, trying to quell her want. It didn't work.

Her life had been one long spiral down, tragedy after tragedy—until now, until Eric and Scott. Hearing Eric call her "little one" and feeling Scott's fingers in her hair awakened something new inside her—hope. Her future had never seemed brighter.

She was about to say "yes," to tell them she was a virgin, when shattering doubt washed away her courage. As much as Eric and Scott had changed her life already, would she be able to be all they needed in a woman? Even though she could see her way around some of the challenges of being with two men at the same time, there were others that still seemed insurmountable, and most of the latter were about her inexperience. Could she honestly be enough for them?

Eric kissed her again, sending her into a delicious state of abandon. When she felt his hands on her breasts, she whimpered into his mouth.

She felt Scott's lips on the back of her neck, the gentleness in his touch making her tingle all over. She was wet and her pussy ached.

Closing her eyes, she melted between them.

Chapter Eleven

Megan's walls were down. Eric's and Scott's kisses and caresses were pressing forward, seizing every one of her thoughts, and crushing every one of her hesitations.

"Let's give her a tour of the playroom, Scott." Eric's voice came from deep within his chest. It rumbled at an octave that vibrated along her skin, raising her temperature.

Scott laid his hand on her arm. "I agree. It's time."

Now. Tell them now. The words were caught in the back of her throat. Why couldn't she get them out? If not now, when?

Eric swept her up into his muscled arms. He smiled when she looked up at him, in what must've been his attempt to calm some of her anxiety. It had the opposite impact on her system, triggering a fresh round of trembles.

Walking out of the kitchen and heading to *that room*, she thought of all the heroines in all her romance books. This must've been how they felt just before surrendering themselves to their lovers. She swallowed hard, trying to dislodge the words that needed to be said, but still nothing.

Hearing their boots echoing from the floor to the walls and ceiling had an odd effect on her, both unsettling and exciting. Why was she having such a difficult time telling them the one thing they needed to know? Maybe if she could start talking about another topic, the more important one—her virginity—would slip out.

"Have either of you had a...a woman...I mean..."

"Are you asking if we've ever fucked solo?" The distinct sarcasm in Eric's voice made her shiver.

She nodded, forcing her eyes to remain on his. "That's right. Have you always shared?"

Scott walked beside them and touched her arm. "Mostly. Only a few times have we done our own thing. Don't worry, sweetheart. If you want either of us one-on-one, I'm happy to comply, and I'm sure so is Eric."

"Agreed, but I'm sure she's excited to have us both at the same time." Keeping a tight hold on her and heading up the stairs, Eric's blue eyes seemed dangerous and kind at the same time. "This will be your first ménage, won't it?"

"Yes," she confessed but held back the full truth. *Now. Say it now. I am a virgin.*

"It's okay, little one," he said. "It's not our first, but I have no doubt it will be our best. We're going to give you an introduction into our lifestyle." Eric's lips curled up into a wicked smile.

She found it suddenly hard to breathe.

"Don't be nervous, sweetheart." Scott opened the door and walked into the room.

"I'm thrilled to bring you here, Megan." Eric carried her to the contraption she'd seen the day she'd arrived at the mansion. "I know what you want and I know what you need."

Scott closed the door.

Eric lowered her slowly to her feet next to the device. Again, he kissed her, adding fuel to her already roaring internal heat.

"What do you know about protocols?"

She recalled some of her steamy books. "You mean safe words?"

"Exactly."

"The submissive—"

"That's you," he stated as a matter of fact.

Juiced palpitations sped through her at his declaration of what role she played here. She was dizzy and floaty, and she loved every bit of it. "I'm to say them to a Dom—"

"Your Doms," Eric corrected.

She nodded as her nerves went into high gear. "My Doms. I'm supposed to say them when I am past my limits."

"Not past." Scott cradled her chin as Eric began gathering up a variety of toys. "Before we get close to your limits. This is your first time with BDSM play, so we expect safe words from you. We're going to use colors."

Crawling with apprehension and expectation, she said, "So 'green' is go, 'yellow' is slow, and 'red' is stop?"

Scott's mouth dropped. "How do you know that?"

"Megan knows more than you can imagine," Eric said, stepping up beside him right in front of her. "She's a reader. Tonight, she's about to become a doer."

How did he know that? *Good guesser, apparently.*

Megan opened her mouth to tell them her truth, but she had to slam it shut when her two Doms went into high gear. She was stripped of her clothes in nothing flat. Unlike on the plane, her panties weren't removed slowly but were tossed to the far corner of the room.

Eric's lurid scan of her body caused her cheeks to burn and her pussy to dampen. Like a well-oiled machine, the duo had her facedown and in cuffs on the bench.

"We want your surrender, little one," Eric said, feathering his lips against her ear.

Scott asked, "What color state are you in now, sub?"

Sub?

The word felt right. With them, and only them, it seemed to fit her to a tee.

Eric and Scott deserved the title of "Dom."

Outside this room, she could be strong, like she'd always been. But in here, she could be vulnerable, embracing everything feminine within her.

She didn't dare glance at either of them, but she couldn't bring herself to answer. It should be so easy to say "green," but it wasn't. She'd read a ton of books about this lifestyle. It was about trust. But that didn't come easy for her, especially still being a virgin.

Did they really want a future with her? She wanted that with them with all her heart. God knew Eric and Scott had changed everything for her. They wanted her right now. She owed it to them to try to be what they needed.

Now. Tell them now.

"Sweetheart, are you okay?" Eric asked. "Do we need to stop?"

She shook her head. "Sorry. Just need a second to catch my breath." And then she immediately followed it with what she'd read in all her books, "Sir."

"You ready to continue your lesson?" Scott asked.

"Yes, Sir."

"That pleases me, baby, more than you know."

Thwack. The slap of Scott's hand on her bare ass shocked her into silence.

"Look at my handprint on her ass," he said.

Eric bent down until she was face-to-face with him. His icy blue eyes were unblinking. "Color?"

"Green, Sir." Her voice, barely more than a whisper, was filled with want. Her pussy clenched and moistened just imagining how she looked to them strapped to this bench.

"Very nice. Again, Scott. Three times." Eric remained right in front of her, a fixture of dominance.

Scott's open hand smacked down on her right ass cheek. *Thwack.* Her clit began to throb and burn terribly. And she got even wetter.

Thwack. The bite of his hand on her other cheek smoldered on her skin like embers.

Thwack. Passionate tears welled up in her eyes as a tremor rolled through her body.

Eric brushed his lips over her face, from her mouth to her nose to her cheeks and even to her eyes. "You're doing great, little one. Three more, Scott."

Vowing to become the kind of woman Eric and Scott deserved,

she braced herself for the next round of pussy-soaking slaps, curling her fingers until her hands were little balled-up fists.

Thwack. Thwack. Thwack.

The arousing heat on her bottom made her lips quiver and her need explode. Eric kissed her on the mouth, devouring her whimpers.

"Color, sub?" Scott asked from above her.

"Green, Sir," she said, hearing her own voice sound tinier and more feminine than she'd ever heard before.

"Three more," Eric said.

Thwack. Thwack. Thwack.

Each slap sent her mind spinning and her body burning. Her pussy screamed for relief, clenching and clenching and clenching again—to the edge of unbearable. Her clit's hot stings pushed her to the brink of sanity, burying her in crushing need. Her senses were sharp and clear, more than they'd ever been. She could feel her body's every sensation, all of them trailing through her like electrical currents—hot, sharp, and shiver-inducing.

Eric touched her cheek, a claiming caress. "I can't wait to feel your pussy tighten around my cock, little one."

She gasped, realizing she'd let this go so far without telling them the truth.

"I think she might like a plug in this pretty ass, bro." Scott's hands cupped her bottom.

Say it now, damn it. Now.

"Have you ever had anal sex before?" Eric asked.

"No, Sir." Swallowing down all her apprehensions, the truth finally dislodged from the back of her throat. "Actually, I've never had sex before. I'm a virgin."

Eric's eyes narrowed. "What did you say?"

She closed her eyes tight, unable to bear looking at his disappointment. "I'm a virgin. I'm a twenty-five-year-old virgin."

Silence.

Her heart thudded with regret. They would toss her aside now.

She would have to return to her dismal life and learn to live with the hole left in her heart brought on by the loss of them, her two cowboys. How? It wasn't possible.

She felt lips on her mouth, Eric's lips. She blinked her eyes wide. Scott was removing the cuffs.

Eric lifted her up in his arms. Scott opened the door.

"Please. I'm so sorry I didn't tell you. I want you to be my firsts. Please."

"Hush, little one," Eric said tenderly.

Scott's face showed both concern and surprise. "Everything is going to be okay, baby."

"Then why are you taking me out of this room?" God, she was tired. Tired of being alone and afraid. Tired of having to fight for everything and still coming up short. Tired of hurting. Tired of seeing Kip's twisted grin every time she closed her eyes. Tired of regret. "I'm tired of being a virgin. Please, can't you understand that?"

"We understand, love," Scott said. "This just isn't the place for you to have your first experience."

"Aren't you even curious why I'm still a virgin?" she asked.

"Not enough to matter right now, little one." Eric's eyes were filled with what seemed to her to be something akin to reverence. "You trusting us with something so precious is the greatest gift we've ever been given. We won't fail you. I promise."

They carried her out of the playroom to her bedroom with the big, comfy bed. Gently, they placed her in the middle of the mattress. Each of them stripped off their clothes. Their cocks were straight up and hard. Did they mean to both make love to her?

"Who is first?" she squeaked out.

"Trust us, Megan."

Scott had a condom wrapper in his hand. He opened it and rolled the latex down his thick, long shaft.

She looked at him and then at Eric. "What about you?"

"Scott's going to take your virginity tonight. I'll take my gift another time, but that doesn't mean I won't be taking a few samples from you. I will." He flashed her another wicked smile. "Tonight is about your pleasure, little one, but believe me, I will be enjoying every whimper, every moan, every scream."

As they each crawled into bed with her, one on each side, nervous shivers took hold of her.

Kisses and caresses rained down every inch of her body. She could feel their cocks pressing into her thighs. These were the kind of men a woman could depend on when needed, a woman like her, and God knew she needed them now in the worst way.

Eric kissed her, cupping the mound of her sex, fingers threading through her wet folds until he touched her aching clit. Scott swallowed her right breast, sucking until her nipple beaded and throbbed. She couldn't keep any part of her body still, fisting the sheets, trying to hold on to the new sensations tearing through her.

When Eric's tongue swept into her mouth, dizziness took hold of her as her pussy burned with a broiling ache. Something strange happened, something she'd only felt recently on the plane with Scott. His teeth tightening on her nipple and Eric's fingers pressing on her clit created a kind of circuit, electric and tingly. Her pussy got even wetter. She was soaked and so very needy. Her thoughts were slippery and unfocused. Reining them into something logical and sensible was impossible at the moment. It was her body that demanded all her attention, her energy, her essence. Sensations ripped through again and again, each hotter and more earth-shattering than the one before.

Her books had told her such a thing was possible, but deep down she'd held on to her doubt, never knowing her body would respond so…so violently.

Scott shifted down her frame, kissing her abdomen as he'd done on the plane. Oral sex was next, thank God. Instinct had taken her over, and her body arched into Scott, trying to fill her unfathomable appetite.

Eric also moved down, leaving her mouth swollen and throbbing from his salacious kiss. He swallowed her other breast, teething her nipple, creating a new zinging line between her breast and her clit, where Scott's tongue was currently circling. Her maddening thirst to be conquered, to be claimed, to be filled, created a bonfire between her legs, skating up her belly and down her thighs. Shivers raced through her. When she felt Scott's tongue hit her clitoris and his two fingers thrust into her pussy to *the spot*, she shot her hands onto both their heads, her left on Eric's and her right on Scott's. She pressed at the back of their heads, hungry for them to consume her, all of her.

Utter devastation coiled through her from their double-teaming efforts—Scott's mouth on her pussy, Eric's on her breast, Scott's tongue swiping across her clit, Eric's across her nipple, Scott's fingers pumping inside her, Eric's tugging her hair.

Nothing inside her could be stilled.

"Please. Please. Please." Her pants filled the room.

"She's ready." Eric pressed his lips to hers, slipping his tongue into her mouth.

Scott kissed his way up her body, pushing her thighs wide with his muscled legs.

Eric released her lips, rolling to the side. "This is it, little one. This is your moment."

She looked deep into his eyes and saw immense tenderness. She turned to Scott, who was now fully on top of her. In his eyes was the same.

She trembled, though trusting them with everything, still a little nervous about what was to happen. She'd never felt so open, so vulnerable, so female.

Scott shifted his hips, positioning the bulbous head of his cock on her sex. He leaned down and swallowed her in an all-important kiss, the last one of innocence.

She closed her eyes, readying herself for the final step, the final drop, the final—

"This is going to hurt at first, little one," Scott said. "But I promise that once the initial pain passes, it will get better. Do you trust me?"

She nodded, chewing on her lower lip.

Scott's smile reassured her. She could feel his love, his caring with every breath and every caress.

"Ready, baby?" Eric asked tenderly.

"Yes, Sir."

Then Scott slipped his cock into her slow and easy. Inch by inch, he went deeper into her pussy as Eric reached between them, pressing on her clit. Her guys were taking their time, clearly hoping to ensure her pain was minimal.

Megan felt a sting and a brief moment of pain. Scott was stretching her beyond what she thought possible, and still his cock went deeper into her flesh. But in a flash, everything inside her, the burn and stretch, morphed into desire. Hot tingles vibrated every inch of her, sweeping her into a state of overwhelming need.

Oh God!

She was screaming into Scott's kisses.

She could feel Eric's sweet caresses in her hair and his fingertips on her clit.

Hot liquid dampened her thighs.

Scott didn't move, didn't breathe. He was a still as a statue.

She moved, couldn't help but move.

Her body frayed at the very edges, and still the pressure went on. She'd dreamed of this, considered every possibility, every nuance, read every book she could get her hands on, but none of it could have prepared her for this.

From the corners of her mind, she was able to make out whispers, whispers to her from Scott and from Eric.

"Megan?" Scott's gentle tone came just as her suffering began to subside.

"Breathe, little one. Holding your breath keeps the pain from releasing. Breathe."

She nodded, keeping her eyes closed, and did as he'd suggested. Her discomfort lessened just as Eric had said it would. She'd never felt anything like this before. Words seemed to fall short of what was going on inside her body. She was forever changed. A threshold had been passed that she could never go back over.

As the sting softened even more, something new took its place, something unrelenting and urgent. She began to shake. Coherent thought was beyond her capacities at the moment.

She opened her eyes, and looked at Scott and Eric.

"She's ready for more, now." Eric looked at his brother and then at her. "Aren't you, little one?"

She nodded and chewed on her lower lip, feeling so tiny and frail.

"Baby, you can't imagine how much it means to me that I was your first." The bead of sweat on Scott's forehead told her he was holding back his monstrous lust with some effort.

"I want to feel more, Scott. Please."

His lips turned up into a hungry grin, and then he began thrusting into her again and again. It still burned but it also stirred a whole new set of sensations she'd never experienced before. They came loaded to the brim with desire, desire to be filled more, to be possessed utterly, to be devastated completely.

"How does it feel, little one? Talk to us."

"Ohhh. God. I feel him inside me," she whispered, then wailed. "Deep. Yes. Really deep. God."

Scott brushed his manly lips on her face and continued to plunge his cock into her pussy. Stroking her hair, Eric dotted her shoulders with gentle kisses, maintaining the press of his fingers on her clit.

"Close. I'm close," Scott whispered against her lips. He thrust into her faster and faster, his lust clearly unleashed and unstoppable.

Eric sucked on her neck. "Come for us, little one. Feel the pleasure. None of us will ever forget tonight."

Unimaginable heat exploded deep in her pussy, spreading out like wildfire through her belly, down her thighs. Her body was overcharged with orgasmic sensations multiplied one on top of another and another and another.

She screamed, melting into Scott's assault, surrendering to his every lust, filling her every need.

More tingles. More shivers. Her climax didn't seem to have an end.

"Fuuuck," Scott shouted.

She could feel his cock pulsing inside her. Her pussy clenched, unclenched, and clenched again on his cock. Her back arched off the bed, and she tugged on their locks in a weak attempt to still her shivers. It didn't work. They came wave after wave, crashing through every nerve, every cell a sea of pulverizing sensations.

Suddenly, Eric cried out. She turned and saw his hot stare on her, his hand on his cock, and his cum on his muscled chest and abdomen. Seeing Eric's release and feeling Scott's ignited another round of climactic trembles inside her.

Passionate tears of release streamed down her face. She felt like the whole world could fade into oblivion as long as she was with Eric and Scott. Whatever came her way, with them she could face anything.

Chapter Twelve

With iPad in hand, Eric sat down at the table on the patio. He was alone at the moment, which gave him a little time to read some e-mails.

The weather was unseasonably warm for this time of day in May. Seventy-three degrees. That must've been the reason Gretchen had set up breakfast outside. The table was filled with the meal he and Scott had enjoyed from time to time from her since they were kids, even before the accident that had taken the lives of their parents.

Gretchen called her breakfast special a two-courser, but it could've been at least ten, and probably was as far as he was concerned, though the entire meal was already set up in a single serving.

Gretchen's first course consisted of fresh-squeezed orange juice and some fresh fruit, today's being sliced strawberries and bananas. He'd learned long ago not to move on to the other items until he'd sampled from number one. Back whenever he did risk a nibble beyond one, her disapproving frown had set him straight.

Course two was the jewel of the meal, a feast of sausages, bacon, eggs, mushrooms, hash browns, and toast with marmalade. Of course, no Gretchen meal was complete without tea.

Megan was still upstairs getting ready for her first day at TBK. Gretchen was with her. Scott should be down shortly.

Eric drank some of his tea and looked at his messages on the iPad. The first was from the technician here in Destiny he'd given Megan's computer and modem to. The kid was young and had been thrilled to be put on a top-secret project for Eric and Scott. The man didn't require many details before diving in, which suited them just fine. Still the tech had nothing useful to report as of his last email.

Eric didn't open the messages from any of the TBK executives, instead deciding to open Dylan's message first. The subject line was too intriguing not to.

"Found K. L."

Kip Lunceford. Dylan had been pulling strings and calling in favors for months to try to locate where the government was keeping him. Had it finally paid off? There was more in Dylan's message that didn't relate to Kip. Vicky was missing with no explanation. She'd been absent from work without so much as a phone call. That wasn't like her. How in the hell had Kip gotten his claws into Vicky? Who was Eric to judge? The bastard had done the same to him and Scott long ago.

Scott walked out onto the patio, his own iPad under his arm. "Gretchen's done it again. I think this is for Megan more than for us."

"I agree. She hasn't made an English breakfast for us in over a month." He reread the e-mail from Dylan. "Got some news here."

"What?"

"Dylan sent you and I an encrypted e-mail. He's found Kip."

"Damn he's good." Scott sat and clicked on his iPad. "Where's Gretchen?"

"I'm betting she's with Megan, helping her pick out the perfect outfit for her first day at TBK."

"I'm sure you're right. I'm glad they hit it off already."

"Was there any doubt?"

Scott shook his head, reading the message on his iPad. "The bastard is in a federal correctional facility in Georgia." Then his brother's jaw dropped. "Shit, Vicky?"

"I know. We should've trusted our instincts about her feelings she'd shown for Kip. It seems she's still into him."

"We don't know that yet. We need proof."

Eric nodded. "I hope you're right and there's a simple explanation for her disappearance. But that's not like her."

Scott sighed. "No, it isn't."

"I'll call Josh and head to Kip's prison after breakfast."

"No." Scott kept his nose in his iPad. "You aren't going, Eric. I am."

"Why not both of us?"

"The only people I would trust Megan's safety to are Emmett, Bryant, Cody, Sawyer, Reed, Josh, or Dylan. The Stones are busy with their new woman, Amber."

"Isn't her name Kathy?"

Scott shrugged, placing his iPad on the table and breaking one of Gretchen's rules by eating the bacon first. "I think Amber is going by the name the guys gave her when she was still suffering from amnesia."

"Makes perfect sense to me."

"Sawyer and Reed are swamped getting ready for the livestock auction in Fort Collins next week. Josh will be flying the plane. Dylan is in DC, according to his e-mail here."

"What about Jason?"

"He's sheriff, bro. He can't give Megan the kind of attention and time we would want from a bodyguard. Besides, he's busy sorting out all that Russian mafia shit that just went down here."

"Agreed," he told Scott. "Why you and not me then? Answer me that."

"Neither of us wants her coming within a hundred miles of that sociopath."

"True." Their former employee was truly a genius, capable of more than he or Scott had ever believed possible. A man they'd once trusted turned traitor to the country they still held dear. Kip had also married Megan and screwed up her life. For that, Eric wanted to kill the bastard.

Scott drained his orange juice in a single gulp. "You and Megan need to spend more time together. I got the trip to New York. Now it's your turn to get to know her better."

Right now, he cared about making sure whatever asshole who'd used her Internet access from her home wasn't still a threat to her. It might be Kip, but it seemed highly unlikely from a federal correctional facility.

"What do you say?" Scott asked.

"You're right." Eric would love to spend some time alone with her. "But besides finding out if Kip is behind the attacks on TBK's system, I want you to ask him one question for me."

"Sure." Scott paused for a sip of tea. "Tell me what question you want me to ask."

"Why was Megan still a virgin after being married to him?"

"That's something I want to know, too. What kind of twisted bastard would do that to such a beautiful, amazing woman like Megan? God, I can't stop thinking about last night, can you?" Scott had a sex drive that had frightened off many a sub.

"No, I can't. But you're going to have to chill, bro."

"What are you talking about?" Scott asked.

"Megan matters to you, doesn't she?"

"Of course." Scott nodded. "She's the one. Agreed?"

"Yes," he confessed. "She is. You're going to have to go more than five minutes without thinking about sex. She's still very scared. We can still blow our chance with her." Eric thought about how Megan must've felt being manipulated by Kip all those years ago. Her innocence. His evil. "Come to think of it don't talk to Kip about Megan. Don't even let him know we have her."

Scott nodded. "I am in complete agreement to your change of plan. He doesn't need to know a fucking thing about Megan." His brother let out a big breath of air. "I won't blow our chance with Megan. I can control myself. Can you?"

Before he could answer, Megan walked onto the patio in an outfit that blasted his yet-unspoken answer "of course, I can control myself" into oblivion. What remained in his head were a million images of

Megan naked and under him.

She looked like a sexy executive with her leather computer bag on her shoulder. Her black pants and top fit her body perfectly, causing his dick to harden in his jeans. The plunging neckline showed just enough of her cleavage to tempt but not enough to make him send her back up to change. No way would he let her be seen in anything more revealing outside without at least a day collar around her neck. A collaring ceremony would have to come later, after a few more lessons. What really caught his attention were her red stilettos. They looked so very sexy on her. They would look even better dangling from her toes hanging down his back while he licked on her pussy, drowning his face in her sweet cream.

"What do you think?" she asked, spinning in a circle, holding her arms out. "It's Christian Dior."

"Very nice." Scott stood and pulled out a chair for her.

"I must agree. What about the shoes?"

"Gretchen picked them out. I had chosen black but she said it was too matchy-matchy. She thought I needed a pop of color. They're Christian Louboutin."

"Gorgeous," he said, unable to shake the image of her underneath him naked and writhing in ecstasy.

"Are you just saying that?" she asked.

"Do you think I would lie to you, little one?"

Her cheeks turned the sweetest shade of pink. "No. I'm sorry. I just am nervous about today. I guess I shouldn't be. I am going into the office with the copresidents of the company."

"Actually, sweetheart, you're going in with Eric. I have another meeting to attend."

Eric didn't like that they were holding back from Megan about Kip, but it was the only way he and Scott believed they could keep her safe. Knowing too much might end in disaster, especially given her immense courage. Megan would want to act, and that was the last thing she needed to do right now.

She frowned. "I'm supposed to be your personal assistant. Shouldn't I be booking your meetings or taking your messages for you?"

"Already claiming your turf, are you?" Scott teased, brushing the hair out of her eyes. "You better eat up. I'm sure Eric is going to work you hard today. And you don't want to disappoint Gretchen. She worked hard on this meal."

"Is there coffee?" she asked.

"Have you heard Gretchen's accent? It's English tea in this house. Nothing else."

She smiled. "Not a problem."

Scott turned to him. "I already got Megan started on the paintball project on the round trip to New York."

"Excellent. Where are you on that?" he asked her.

She needed to feel valued, and the truth was that project was an important one for TBK and for Scott and him, too.

Megan smiled and pulled out her new laptop. She turned it on. "I've got some questions about that, if you two don't mind."

"Can we clone her, Scott? An army of her in all our offices would double our company's value."

"What do you mean?" she asked.

"It's not even seven and you're already on the job."

"I'm excited to get started, Eric." She looked at her screen. "I pulled up the website for Destiny's Annual Paintball Extravaganza this morning. The proceeds are earmarked for children's charities chosen by a board of ten citizens. Who is on the board?"

"This year's list includes Ethel O'Leary, Jennifer Steele, Cody Stone, Phoebe Blue, Melissa and Hiro Phong, Lucy and Norman, and me and Scott."

Gretchen came in with a suitcase. "Scott, I understand you have a trip to make today."

"If I didn't know better, I would think you might be behind our hacker problem at TBK. How did you know that? I just found out myself not ten minutes ago."

Even as children, she'd dazzled them with her ability to be ready for anything. She deserved a merit badge for her talents.

"I'm a witch and we don't tell our secrets. You should know that after all these years, young man."

"Especially not your real age," Eric said.

Gretchen laughed and then scanned the table. "Not hungry? Surely I didn't get up at four to get this all ready for you to have it go to waste?"

He grinned. "Master manipulator, that's who you are, Mrs. Hollingsworth."

"Mind your tongue and eat."

"Are you going to join us, Gretchen?" Megan asked.

Eric was about to tell her that Gretchen never had a meal with them no matter how much they begged her when something shocking happened.

"I think I will, dear." Gretchen pulled up a chair to a plate of food he hadn't even noticed before. It was a smaller plate than all the rest but filled with tinier portions of the same meal. She had intended to eat with them all along.

Eric looked over at Scott, who by the strip of bacon hanging from his unmoving mouth must've been just as taken aback by this as he was.

"Stop gawking at me, boys. Eat."

"Yes, ma'am," Scott said, gobbling up the strip of bacon.

"When does the board choose a recipient of the monies from the paintball event?" Megan was back on task. He liked how focused she could be when necessary.

"Usually a couple months after the bout," he told her. "No later than August, though."

Scott's plate was empty. "If I were a betting man, I'd put my chips on the new Boy's Ranch the Stone brothers are setting up for Amber's orphans."

"You are a betting man," Gretchen said. "The weekly poker game at the O'Learys' is something you two never miss."

"Nor do you," Scott teased.

"Guilty as charged," the dear woman answered.

Megan looked at him with her green eyes, which were glistening in the morning light. "What about my old computer? Did you find anything on it?"

Eric shook his head and saw the disappointment spread over her face.

"I know you've never said this is connected to Kip in some way, but it is, isn't it?"

Time to distract her. "Megan, let's get back to the paintball event. You're going to have to coordinate with the sheriff and his deputy for security. TBK and O'Leary Enterprises provide additional support on that front, being cosponsors of the event."

"I'm not an idiot, Eric. Talk to me. What are you guys working on to get to the bottom of all of this mess?"

Scott told her their entire plan before Eric could stop him. "Baby, we've put in some code and false information that should smoke out any mole inside TBK."

"Do you think that will lead you to Kip or whoever is working with him?" The five-year struggle she'd gone through was evident in every sigh. "I'm not even sure he's still in prison."

"Who knows where he is?" Eric hated lying to her, knowing full well Kip's actual location since Dylan's e-mail. But he felt that was the best course to take with her for now. "Besides, Megan, if the asshole is in prison there's no way he's involved with our issues." Eric knew better, but didn't want to add to her worries. He and Scott knew firsthand how capable Kip could be at manipulation, which was only surpassed by the brilliant asshole's computer skills.

"We've got a short list of suspects that we're going through." Scott pushed his empty plate forward, and then shot Eric a glance that let him know he, too, wanted to change the subject off of Kip.

"And they are?" Megan wasn't backing down. He couldn't blame her after all the hell she'd gone through because of Kip.

"Vicky Bates currently tops the list," Eric told her. "She's an exec at our company but has recently gone missing."

"Did Kip ever work with her?" Megan asked, once again turning the conversation back to the person who had ruined her life.

"Yes," Scott said. "Kip and Vicky were part of the first group we hired at TBK years ago."

"Any other questions, sweetheart?" he asked, allowing a hint of irritation to show in his tone.

It was important to keep Megan busy for many reasons, but the most important being to keep her mind off of finding the hacker. That was his and Scott's job, not hers.

"Just don't leave me in the dark, guys."

"Trust us, sweetheart," he told her. Not a lie but definitely not the truth either. "Now let's get back to working out the details about the paintball event."

Megan nodded.

* * * *

Megan walked out the door of The Knight Mansion with Eric. "Is it just me or is the weather getting even better?"

"It is." Eric was still a mystery to her.

Last night had been the best night of her life. She had lost her virginity to Scott, and in a way to Eric, too. They'd changed her completely. She felt so alive, maybe for the first time in her life. She was still a little sore from her first time. God, it had happened and it had been more than she'd ever dreamed. Of course it was. The Knights were experienced Doms. They knew their way around a woman's body better than the average man, and probably better than most Doms.

Could she be enough for Eric? For Scott? Last night had been life changing, but they'd carried her out of their special sanctum because they didn't think she could handle it. Megan's doubts screamed and mocked her like they always did. Best to think about something else than lose herself in a tornado of crazy thoughts.

"How many employees work at the TBK offices?"

"Around the country? Six hundred thirty-three."

"Wow. That's pretty exact, Eric."

"It's important to me to be exact." He stopped at the top of the stairs. "Look at those mountains, little one."

Little one. Why did her knees want to buckle every time he called her that? "They're beautiful."

"Let's walk to the office today."

"Sounds wonderful. How far is the building?" She hadn't gotten to get a good view of the street their mansion was on the day they'd brought her here, being so nervous about their proposal.

"Two blocks. Five-minute walk. Ten-minute saunter."

Saunter wasn't a word she heard often back in Dallas. It bespoke of an earlier age, an age of gallantry, which Eric had by the bucketloads.

They walked past his car and down the drive to the road, which ran between the Knights' place and another mansion across the street. "Who lives there?"

The place was ultramodern in styling, like giant blocks with walls of glass, and what parts of the walls weren't see-through were crisp white. In front of the place was a long rectangle pond. She couldn't see it from here, but she would bet there were koi in lots of the glass and crisp white walls. The landscaping had a cool Asian feel.

"Number Two, O'Leary Circle. Jennifer Steele does."

"Alone?"

"She lost her husband Bill to cancer twelve years ago."

"Any kids?"

"Bill had a daughter from a previous marriage, but I've never met the girl. I don't think she and Jennifer get along."

"Sounds like she's had a tough time." Money might make someone's life easier, but obviously heartbreak was the universal leveler whether rich or poor.

"Jen is tough. She's the unattached queen of the subs at Phase Four. She's gotten many offers by Doms to take their collar, but she has refused them all."

"Collar?" she asked.

"Part of the life."

"Like a wedding ring?"

Eric nodded. "And more."

Megan could just imagine what the "more" meant. "I'm not surprised men wouldn't want someone who has a place like this." She pointed to the massive house. Looking to her right, she saw the road came to a dead end. "I see we go left."

"We do." Eric could be a man of few words at times. At other times, he could be quite talkative, like when he was with Gretchen.

The grade was uphill, and she wondered if she should've worn tennis shoes instead of stilettos. As they walked up the road, they came to the circle that gave the name to the whole lane. The mansion that bordered it was massive, four stories high. It looked more like a gothic castle than anything she'd ever seen before. Of course, the massive dragon statue in front of it told her who resided inside.

"And that is Number One, O'Leary Circle." Eric smiled, which was not common for him. "Ethel, Patrick, and Sam live there." His tone reminded her of how he talked to Gretchen, laden with affection.

"It looks like it could use a moat."

He stopped walking and stood in the middle of the street, facing the fairy-tale place. "Don't tease. Patrick has plans drawn up for one, but Ethel has put her foot down."

"How big is it inside?"

"Twenty-two thousand square feet."

"Wow. That's impressive."

"You should see inside. They hold the four big seasonal events for

Destiny—Summer Solstice on June twenty-first, Halloween, which costumes are required, a Christmas party that will blow your mind, and Dragon Week, which is celebrated in March."

"Dragon Week? The O'Learys are crazy for dragons, aren't they?"

"Just Patrick. Ethel tolerates it, but Sam, his brother, loves to rib him about it every chance he gets."

"Why is Mr. O'Leary so passionate about dragons anyway?"

"You'll have to ask him yourself. I want to see your face when he tells you." Eric touched her cheek. "We better get going. You don't want to be late on your first day."

"I hear the boss is a tyrant."

"You hear right. Let's go."

They turned left, continuing their morning walk.

The circle connected the two parts of the street together. The one that was between The Knight Mansion and The Steele Estate ran east and west. The one that connected the exclusive neighborhood to the rest of the town ran north and south.

At the intersection of North and East Streets, Eric stopped again. "What do you think of our downtown, Megan?"

Why did everyone who lived here have such pride about this place? Maybe it was because Destiny was unlike anywhere else in the world. Most likely.

"It's beautiful." She glanced at the dragon statue on the opposite corner from where they stood. Phoebe had called it The Red Dragon. Passion. The memories of last night swirled in her head, and she felt her body suddenly start tingling. She glanced over at Eric, who was staring at her with his intense blue eyes.

"Red Dragon is something, isn't she?"

"I thought it was a he?"

He shrugged. "I guess it depends on your perspective, little one."

Don't fail me, knees. Not now. Not here.

Chapter Thirteen

Scott sat on a bench facing a prison cell similar to one he'd seen in a movie, only in this version he was in the role Foster played. Kip Lunceford was the stand-in for Hopkins.

Kip hadn't changed much in the last five years, same dark hair, ears tipped out slightly at the top, and blue-gray eyes. Six foot tall, he stood at the back of his cell leaning against the wall. His clothes were different, though, prison orange.

Calling in a favor, Dylan had only gotten him ten minutes with Kip. The facility in Atlanta was a maximum-security prison, but they'd still built an area just for Kip. The gruesome details of what had happened in the years after the traitor was taken from Megan's home were in the file beside Scott.

After Kip's conviction, the feds had sent him to Beckley, West Virginia, to a medium-security facility. It made sense to them since his crimes were nonviolent in nature back then.

Kip had the run of the place in less than a week, controlling the entire prison's computer system from a terminal in the prison library. After a few months, Kip had started using his unique access to open exit doors, turn off surveillance cameras, and leave without the on-duty guards' knowledge.

The FBI had no suspects and no leads for the seven connected murders of gay men in the Beckley area for over a year until by happenstance the prison's computer system came up for an audit. A talented technician named Paula Childs, a single mother of three, noticed some discrepancies. The lead auditor on the project told her to move on, but the woman couldn't let it go. She found the evidence that proved Kip had been leaving the prison whenever he felt like it.

In less than three days, the FBI had solved the case. Kip was the serial killer. The creep had confessed with a smirk. When asked why he'd committed such horrific crimes, Kip had flippantly told them he'd done it because he could and was bored. The prison psychiatrist's notes on his sessions with Kip were gruesome. Things like "I loved seeing them beg for their lives" and "there's nothing like seeing a worthless wretch scream their last breath" were just a couple of the heinous words of the madman documented in the file. The one that stuck out the most to Scott was the final entry in the shrink's records. "Trust me, Doc. If I ever get bored again, I've a got a long list of scum to take care of and there's no prison that can hold me."

Since West Virginia abolished the death penalty in 1965, Kip received seven back-to-back life sentences, which went on top of his previous life sentence for a total of eight.

Kip was moved to a high-security prison in Marion, Illinois. He was not allowed to use any of the computers in the place, as the warden feared he might do what he'd done in Beckley. The warden had been smart to worry. One of the guards gave him a cell phone. With it, Kip broke into the prison's network, taking it over as he'd done before. The guard's bank account suddenly had over three hundred thousand dollars deposited into it from an offshore source that the FBI, to this day, hadn't been able to track down.

Kip left Marion for a suburb of Chicago, where Paula Childs had just relocated with her kids. Paula was shot in the head twice and in the chest once. The kids, thankfully, had been away at their grandparents'.

Kip had returned to Marion and confessed to the crime without hesitation or remorse. The next psychiatrist noted how much the bastard loved talking about the murders. It was like a badge of honor to him, a way of proving how superior he was to everyone around him.

He was then moved to a high-security prison, which it turned out had been by his design to end up there. He'd forged some records that weren't found out until later. Even without access to computers, cell phones, or anything else and with only an hour a day out of his cell, he'd figured a way around the system. Kip had gotten one of his cronies hired on at the new prison as a guard six months before his arrival. With the help of his plant, in no time, Kip was the kingpin of the inmates. Unlike before, Kip only left that prison one time, killing two more people—his mother and father.

His final confession might've been the worst of the lot. "You can't imagine how satisfying it was to see their eyes wide with shock when their loving and brilliant son slit their wrinkled throats."

That was eighteen months ago. The warden at this prison was taking no chances with Kip, the reason for the unique cell.

"How's your brother?" Kip asked behind the thick Plexiglas wall.

"I'm not here to get reacquainted. I'm here to ask you some questions." Keeping his rage in check was proving difficult.

Megan had been conned into marrying Kip. If the fucker hadn't been arrested soon after, Kip might've hurt or even killed her. Thank God the bastard would spend the rest of his miserable life in this tiny cell.

"You wouldn't happen to have a motherboard on you, Scott? An old friend could sure use some help right now."

"We're not friends."

"We were once."

"I was a friend to you. You used Eric and me. You were never a real friend."

"I'm sorry you see it that way, Scott. I see it entirely from a different vantage point, a more enlightened vantage point, I might add."

God, Scott had forgotten how arrogant the bastard could be. "The clock is ticking and I have a few questions."

"It's ticking for you, Scott. Not me. I remember how you and Eric always liked making the big deals. Here's my offer, take it or leave it.

Twenty questions each where only 'yes' or 'no' is the answer. I go. Then you go. And so on. Do we have a deal?"

"Like the kids' game?"

Breaking the rules and beating the odds had always been Kip's fascination. Nothing had changed. It had only gotten worse.

"You're right. We're not kids anymore. We're all grown up. Seven questions then. Do we have a deal?"

Fuck! The creep was enjoying this. Getting what he'd come for would be difficult with the limitations Kip had set up.

As tough as it might be, he would have to try. "Yes. But that was your first question."

Kip laughed. "Bingo. Now you."

Scott took a deep breath, trying to formulate the right first question. Kip surely couldn't be the one getting in the back door of TBK's network. But what if he was? *Best to start with the obvious.* "Are you the one hacking into TBK's network?"

"No. Now, my turn. Are you fucking my wife?"

Scott's blood boiled to blistering hot. He'd made it a point not to mention Megan. He didn't want Kip to have any clue about her. "What do you know about Megan?"

Kip made a buzzing sound like heard on TV game shows when someone gives a wrong answer. "You just lost two questions, one for not answering my question and one for asking a question that couldn't be answered by 'yes' or 'no.' You're down to four. But as a courtesy, I'll answer what I know. I married Megan because she was pretty and gullible."

Scott would love nothing more than to get on the other side of that glass and make the world a better place by executing the psycho with his bare hands. "Stop playing games with me, Kip."

"The poor thing holds a special place in my heart, Scott. She kept trying to find me in the prison system after my arrest. I'm sure she wanted to sue me for divorce, but I wasn't having any of that. It was easy for me to manipulate the prison records and send her on wild-goose chases."

"I know where you are now and she will be divorcing you."

Kip shrugged. "Okay. I was bored with that little game a long time ago. When can I expect to see my wife with the divorce papers?"

Scott pounded on the Plexiglas. "Never. Answer my questions and I'll leave you alone."

"What makes you think I want to be alone?"

Scott made the same buzzing sound. "Can't answer that according to your own rules."

"I was testing you and you passed with flying colors. Very good." Kip's condescending tone didn't matter to him. "I'll be a sport and mark me down to four, also. It's a dead heat. Your turn."

"Let's cut the crap and you tell me what you know."

"Too bad. I guess we're done here then."

"The fuck we are."

Kip's lips twisted into a sinister smile. "That's the Scott Knight I remember, the brother who has trouble with control. Very nice. I always considered myself an amalgam of you and Eric. Your passion melded with his control. Of course, my brains are my own. Sorry."

"You're nothing like us and we're most certainly nothing like you."

"Do you have a question for me or are you forfeiting?"

Scott tamped down the murderous storm inside him. Four questions. "Do you know who is hacking into TBK?"

"Excellent. The answer is 'yes.'"

His gut tightened. Kip might not be the hacker but he knew who was.

"My turn," the asshole said. "Is Vicky still working at TBK?"

Why would Kip ask about Vicky? "Do you know where she is?"

"No. Pretty girl."

The fucker was clearly lying. But how could he have any contact to the outside being in this kind of cell? Hoping to push him into slipping up, Scott said, "The feds think you're gay. Vicky was into you as I recall and you didn't give her the time of day. Makes sense to me."

"Gay. Straight. Just labels for people who can fit into neat little boxes all together. I'm unique, Scott. You are, too, you know."

"If you're trying to give me a compliment, don't. Besides, looks to me like they found a box that can hold you."

Kip frowned and narrowed his eyes, revealing he hadn't figured a way out of this cell as he had the others. "Your turn, cowboy."

"Is the hacker working at TBK?"

"Yes. Was Megan's pussy nice and tight the first time you fucked her?"

"You goddamn motherfucker." He stood and pounded on the glass with his fists.

Kip smiled. "Too bad. That insult lost you the rest of your questions. I'm bored with this. The game is over, Scott, but I do hope to see you again."

"The game is hardly over." He grabbed up the files on the bench and exited.

* * * *

Megan looked across the street at the O'Leary Tower, a ten-story office building featuring a projecting cornice decorated with interlocking circles and leafy garlands.

"Tallest building in Destiny. TBK's offices are behind it."

"Impressive. Looks like you could plop it down in any major city in the country and it would fit right in. Looks turn of the century."

"Patrick and Sam would love hearing that. It was built in 1976, but they wanted it to look as if it had been in town for a hundred years. I'll have to let them know it worked."

They crossed over South Street continuing down East. When she spotted the marble inlay of a dragon above the entrance of the tower, she grinned. She really couldn't wait to meet the eccentric Patrick

O'Leary.

A few steps more and she saw TBK's building come into view. It sat next to the O'Leary Tower and was as different from it as night and day. It looked like a giant mirrored box.

"Ta-da," Eric said with a grin. "Welcome to TBK Destiny."

"I wasn't sure what to expect, but this is beautiful. Be honest, you had more say in the design than Scott."

"Damn, there's little that gets past you. Yes. Scott's been the lead on all the other TBK locales' architecture. He built the mansion, so when we decided to put a building in our hometown, I took charge."

"It's so different from your home."

"Come on inside. You'll recognize Scott's input here and there." Eric took her hand and squeezed. "But it is mostly me in there."

They walked into the building through the massive glass doors. To their left a guard sat behind a large desk, also made of glass. A small reception area with white leather modern sofas sat opposite him. Another set of doors, also of glass but this time frosted so she couldn't see beyond, stood right in front of them.

"Hello, Mr. Knight."

"Terrence, how are you?"

"I'm fine. I have Mrs. Lunceford's badge right here, just as you requested." Terrence handed him a plastic card.

"Thanks." Eric gave it to her. "This grants you access into the building." He waved good-bye to the guard and led her to the door. "All you have to do is swipe your badge like this." He took his own card and demonstrated. She heard a buzzing noise. Eric pulled the door open. "Time to clock in, little one."

Stepping through the door, she gasped at the beauty in the massive open space. It looked like a piece of art. The walls reminded her of paper origami in several shades of white, seeming to fold and twist into itself. Clean lines in the furnishing and indirect lighting gave a sense of order. There were no cubicles here but tidy workspaces with large monitors, three to a person. It looked more like a science fiction spaceship than an office.

"I don't see Scott's influence here."

"Good eye. Let's get you settled in."

"I'd like that. There's an empty desk over there by the window."

Eric put his arm around her. "This isn't your floor, little one."

He led her to the bank of elevators. "Try your card on the reader, Megan."

"You have to use your card to use the elevator here at TBK?"

"The projects we work on are sensitive. The higher the floor, the greater the sensitivity and the more clearance and background checks are required."

"Have you run a background check on me?"

"No need. Dylan got the scoop on you when we were trying to sue you. You're clean."

She swiped her card and the elevator doors opened. They walked in.

Eric punched the top-floor button. When the elevator stopped, the door didn't open immediately. A voice came through a speaker. "This is the executive level. Please swipe your card and enter your access code number on the keypad below for entry to this level."

"You weren't kidding about security, Eric."

"I wasn't. There's more. You'll see. Only TBK execs and a few other employees can reach this floor. Scott and I are the only TBK executives in Destiny. Well, now you."

"I'm not an executive, Eric. I'm your personal assistant." *For three months?* She'd forgotten about the time frame in all the swirl of the past couple of days. That was the contract. No more. No less. Her gut tightened at the thought.

"Whatever," he said with a laugh. "Your badge works here, too. I gave you the same number as mine. Later, you'll need to pick your own number. Right now, mine is synced to your badge. Zero-nine-two-eight-two-zero-zero-one. Try it again."

The card reader was just above the keypad. She swiped it as

instructed.

"Perfect," he said. "Now the keypad."

She entered the numbers by memory. "That's a date, right?"

"It is."

"Welcome, Megan, to TBK," the voice said, and then the doors opened.

"I've seen this kind of thing in the movies but not in real life."

"I'm glad you're impressed," he said.

They stepped out of the elevator to the top floor. Here was Scott's influence. Warmer tones. Softer furnishings.

"Hello, Eric," a buxom brunette said from behind a big desk right to their left.

"Hey, Erica."

Erica? You've got to be kidding.

"You must be Megan." The woman came around the desk and held out her hand.

She shook Erica's hand. "Must be nice sharing a name with the boss."

"It beats changing my name to Scott. Too masculine, don't you think?" Erica winked, and Megan's green-eyed monster scurried to the back of her consciousness to remain on guard.

"Eric. Erica. Doesn't it get confusing?"

"Not really. Sometimes, I guess. Just remember I'm the one with the deep voice." Erica laughed, and Megan was beginning to think she might actually like spending time with her. "I love your outfit. It's gorgeous."

"Thank you." She looked at Erica's attire. White blouse, silver earrings and necklace, tan slacks, and high heels. "Yours, too."

"Got to love TBK's wardrobe allowance, don't you?" She lowered her voice in a conspiratorial tone. "Don't tell Eric or Scott, but I'd work here for free if I had to as long as I got to keep it."

"We already know that about you, Erica. It's cheaper to give you the allowance than to pay you what you're really worth."

"You can say that again," the woman said. "All the executives are online for the video staff meeting. Only one slot missing, Felix, who is supposed to be filling in for Vicky."

"Why?" Eric asked her.

She shrugged. "Felix called in sick."

Eric raised one dark eyebrow. Something clearly didn't sit right about this for him. "Felix has one of the best attendance records in all of TBK. Strange."

"Don't be paranoid, boss," Erica said. "Felix is older than when he started with you guys. Maybe he's ill."

Megan wondered what was going thorough Eric's mind.

"Maybe," he said. "I'll head to the conference room in a minute after I get Megan settled in." Eric pulled out his cell. "I'm going to call Felix at home."

"I could do that for you," the woman said.

"I didn't ask you, did I?" After hitting Felix's number, he brought his cell to his ear.

Erica snorted. "No, you didn't. But do you mind keeping your Dom demeanor off this floor. That works at Phase Four but not here. I'm your employee, not your sub."

Eric glared at her. He definitely didn't care for her insolence. "Damn. Voicemail." He hung up his phone.

The woman glared back in clear defiance for a moment, but in only a few seconds looked away.

"Let the GMs know I'll be there shortly," Eric said. "Megan, you're with me."

"Okay."

Eric led her to another set of double frosted-glass doors. "These are our offices. Mine. Scott's. Yours." He pointed to the box by the door with another keypad. "This is the latest biometrics technology."

"I'm not familiar with that."

"Think of a fingerprint. No two are alike, but it's not that difficult to fake fingerprints if you know what you're doing. Like fingertips, our eyes are unique, too, and in particular the iris. This scans your eye and runs an algorithm that analyzes features in the colored tissue surrounding your pupil. It compares rings, furrows, and filaments. All you have to do is look into the device here." He pointed to an eyepiece on the box. "This model has a cool feature in that it runs several scans in a microsecond with a variety of illuminations to prevent a false positive."

"You love this stuff, don't you?" She could hear the excitement in his voice.

"Yes. I'm a geek."

A very sexy geek who looks more cowboy in his Stetson and boots than a billionaire technocrat.

"This same model is used at the Pentagon." He leaned down, moving his eye within a few inches of the eyepiece.

"Welcome, Eric. Please enter your numeric code on the keypad now."

"Same one as the elevator?" she asked.

He nodded and typed in the number.

"September 28, 2001. What's the significance?"

The doors opened silently on their own.

She thought that was very cool, very sci-fi.

"It's the day my parents died in the plane crash. Come on in."

Shocked at his sudden openness to her, Megan felt her pulse race as they walked in. The doors closed behind them. She heard the hidden locking mechanism activate.

"Let's get a picture of your eye so that you can open the doors on your own. This is the most secure space in the building. The walls and doors are made from the best bullet-resistant material on the market."

"What market? Not Walmart or Target."

"No. But it is the best."

She looked around the room, which was a blend of the brothers' opposing tastes. Two desks sat opposite each other. "That's yours." She pointed to the glass and chrome desk and futuristic chair.

"It is."

She turned to look at the other. That desk was dark mahogany with a tufted black leather chair. Very traditional. Very Scott.

"Follow me," Eric ordered, in a tone she was coming to crave.

"Yes, Sir." She followed him to his desk. Five monitors. "Can I call the International Space Station from here?"

"Why?" He sat in his chair and typed something onto his keyboard. It wasn't actually a keyboard, but an image of a keyboard reflected on his mirrored desktop. "Is there an astronaut I should be worried about?"

She laughed and he smiled.

"Time to turn your eye into a key, little one." He placed a metal box similar to the one outside and also with an eyepiece on his desk. "All you have to do is place your eye about an inch from here." He tapped the end of the eyepiece. "I'll snap some pictures and we're done."

Old memories about her mother resurfaced, making her hesitate. "If I'm not with you or Scott, couldn't Erica let me in?"

He shook his head. "Only three people have access to this space—me, Scott, and Gretchen. You will make the fourth person."

"Gretchen?"

He smiled. "She insisted. There's times when we work through the night. She brings us meals. Besides, would you tell her 'no' about anything?"

Megan smiled. "Whatever Gretchen wants, Gretchen gets."

"Now you're talking. Until we figure out who is behind the cyber attacks and also used your IP at your home, you will be with either me or Scott at all times when we are at TBK. If we have to go, like I do now to conduct the videoconference, you will stay in here. Understand?"

"Then I don't need to scan my eye. I'm either with you or I'm already in here. See what I mean?"

"Why are you nervous about this?" he asked.

"It's my eyes." She then confessed, "My mother went blind six months before she died from complications to her chemo. I'm a little jittery when it comes to my eyes. Thank God, I have twenty-twenty vision. I could never wear contacts."

Eric placed his hand over hers. "Indulge me this, Megan. It's only a picture."

"Okay. I think you're being overprotective, but I'll go through with it if it makes you happy."

"It does."

"What do you think will happen? A bunch of bandits will charge in here and you and Scott will take them on while I run into this *safe place?*"

He cupped her chin. "Less than a week ago, Destiny had a shootout with the Russian mafia just a block from here. People were killed. I'm a guy who likes to be prepared. You matter to me very much, Megan Lunceford. Do this for me."

"Okay." She leaned down and felt his fingers stroking her hair, working to soothe her fears some.

In less than ten seconds, he was done. "I've got all I need, little one. You're all set."

"That's it?"

"Yep. You'll learn to trust me."

"I do trust you, Eric." Her heart thudded in her chest.

"Eric, I've got the sheriff on the line. He wants to know if you have time to take a call?" Erica's voice came from some hidden speakers near the desk.

He clicked on one of the button images on his desktop. "I'll be there in sixty seconds."

He stood up and pulled her into his muscled frame. "You better get started on the paintball project. Use my desk. I'll be back in about an hour." And then he kissed her, making her toes curl and her belly flip-flop.

And then he was gone.

The doors closed and she heard the lock engage. She pulled out her new laptop and placed it on Eric's desk.

As Megan turned it on and it started to boot up, she felt a smile spread across her face.

* * * *

The rental car left the highway for the road to Destiny, Colorado, a place not unfamiliar to its driver, but this trip was for an entirely different reason than all the rest. Megan the bitch was there. *She's fucked up my life for the last time.* How she'd won over the Knight brothers so easily was a mystery.

Time to get back the modem that had been planted at her house. Not difficult now with access to the top floor of TBK's building in the tiny town.

The gun in the passenger seat would solve everything. Soon it would be over. Really over.

Chapter Fourteen

Megan finished typing in the security assignments for Destiny's Annual Paintball Extravaganza. Charlie Blake, Jason's deputy, was going to be in charge of most of it. Everyone in town was sad about him tendering his resignation to Jason but most understood why. Charlie's ex had moved to California with his kids. He couldn't bear being so far from them, so he was moving there at the end of the summer.

Megan was falling in love with Destiny and its citizens with each passing day. They were quirky in so many ways but they had the biggest hearts she'd ever known.

This was her second day at TBK and Megan was getting into the swing of things. Eric and Scott had brought a desk for her into TBK's Presidential Fortress of Solace, which she had learned was the term used by the employees, including their executive secretary Erica, who wasn't afraid to say it to the copresidents' faces.

She'd grown so fond of Erica. She had real moxie and a mouth on her that made Eric cringe and Scott laugh. The jealousy she'd felt for the girl was unwarranted. She was like a sister to the brothers. Her parents had died in the same plane crash as Eric and Scott's. The tragedy of September twenty-eighth had hit the town of Destiny hard, leaving eight teenagers from three families orphaned. It was clear to her now that there was quite a bond between Erica and the Knights. She would bet the same bond existed with all the orphans. Erica's brothers, Sawyer and Reed, worked on the Stone Ranch, which was owned by three other orphans, Emmett, Bryant, and Cody.

It was about lunchtime, when the guys said they would be back.

She was getting tired of being left alone in the PFS, as she liked to refer to it, but both Eric and Scott demanded she stay put whenever they had to be away. She was to open the door to no one. Strict orders.

PFS had its own bathroom complete with shower, whirlpool bath, and the plushest towels she'd ever felt on her fingertips. There was a kitchenette and coffee bar that she'd raided twice already. Eric and Scott worked hard and long hours. She'd hoped to have a repeat of the other night when they'd made love to her, but there'd been no time. The hacker was still on the loose. Between the three of them, she bet they'd slept less than eight hours in the past three nights combined.

She heard the lock disengage, and for the oddest reason, her body tensed. Why? The truth was she was nervous knowing whoever had used her Internet access at her home was still on the loose. She might feign aggravation to Eric and Scott about how overprotective they were, but actually she was glad for it.

When Eric and Scott walked in, her shoulders relaxed. When she saw Jason, Destiny's sheriff, follow them in, her tension returned. All their faces looked grim.

"Hey, sweetheart," Scott said. "We won't be but a few minutes, and then we can go to the diner for lunch."

"What's wrong? Did you find Kip?"

"We did, but that's not what this is about," Scott said.

"You found him? When? Where?"

"Shh. There's other fish to fry."

A sudden bout of nausea hit her. "Don't give me that, Scott Knight." Her heart was thudding in her chest like a rapid-fire gun. "I deserve to know."

Jason said, "Do you need a moment, fellows?"

"When did you find Kip?" she asked again.

"I'll step out," the sheriff said.

"That would be great. This will only take a minute." Eric's tone had the edge that made her tremble. He clicked the button on the wall behind her desk that unlocked the door.

The sheriff exited.

Eric walked to one side of her and Scott walked to the other.

She stood up and slapped her hands on the top of her desk. "Did you lie to me or not?" She could feel the manic tornado inside her grow stronger and stronger. *I'm an idiot when it comes to men.* The mantra swirled over and over in her head, crushing her into a million pieces of despair.

Eric leaned down. She turned her head to the side, refusing to be sidetracked by his kiss. Then she felt a sharp tug on her hair. She turned and saw it was Scott, not Eric, who had pulled her locks.

She glared at him. "Liars."

Eric pinched her nipples, delivering a sharp sting. "Enough, sub." His words were like a slap to her bottom, and her manic thoughts slowed.

Tears welled up in her eyes. "I don't understand. How could you do this to me?"

"Do what exactly?" Eric's tone was steady but firm. "Be clear."

His fingers remained lightly on her now-throbbing nipples, but she knew he would clamp down on her bits of flesh whenever Eric deemed necessary.

"Why didn't you tell me you found him? I'm still his wife. I've been trying to find him for five years."

"Why were you looking for him, little one?" Eric's tone was softer than before but still just as demanding.

"To divorce him, of course."

"That's already in the works, sweetheart," Scott said. "He's in prison. He can't get to you, but he's more dangerous than any of us imagined."

"What do you mean?"

"He's a serial killer, little one," Eric answered. "Scott went to see him the day you first came to work at TBK. That was his meeting in Georgia. Kip is in prison in Atlanta."

"I don't understand why you didn't tell me then. Don't you trust me?"

"Should we? You don't trust yourself yet. Do you?"

It was true. She didn't.

"Everything we've done, Megan, has been to protect you," Eric said. "Time to come completely clean. I went to your house and got your modem when you were in New York with Scott. That, too, was to protect you."

She was mortified that he'd been in her house, her mother's house. The condition it was in was horrific. "I'm so confused about all of this."

"Kip is in jail, but he's had reach to the outside before and we believe he might have it again. There was no way we wanted you near him. If we told you, you would've wanted to see him, yes?"

She nodded, recalling how hard she'd tried to locate Kip to hand him divorce papers.

"Not possible. And we didn't want you to have to struggle with knowing that. You've been through too much. We are cleaning things up. You'll get your divorce. That's what I want. That's what Scott wants. And you? What do you want?"

"I want that, too."

"You've got to learn to trust us," Scott said.

"And yourself." Eric brushed the hair out of her eyes. "Just because Kip conned you doesn't mean you don't deserve happiness."

"Please wait." Megan needed them to understand why, needed them to hear her story. "Hear me out, please, Sirs," she added, hoping her submissive words would soften them.

Eric leaned against her desk, releasing her nipples. "Okay. Talk to us."

She placed her head into his chest and let the tears fall. "Kip came into my life at my lowest point. My mother had died two months earlier. My grief was overwhelming. I wanted to die. Enter Kip, a charming, handsome guy who distracted me away from my sadness.

He's smart, maybe even a genius."

"We know, sweetheart." Scott reached over and touched her cheek. "He's also a fucking murderous nut, genius or not."

"This is the twenty-first century. I thought the closet was a thing of the past, but Kip showed me I was wrong. There are still holdouts in every part of this country that cling to bigotry. Kip knew that better than most." The old memories rushed out of her like a flood, each syllable carrying ancient black pain, and with them, tears.

Eric kissed her tears. "Keep going, little one. You're doing great."

"One month of seeing me and he knew my weakness, my kryptonite. Men. I'm an idiot when it comes to men. He proposed." Her words came in breathy shudders.

"Tell us, baby," Scott said, urging her on with gentle words.

"I thought Kip actually cared for me. I even thought I had feelings for him. Even at twenty, I should've known better, but I didn't. I said 'yes.' Next thing I know we're in Las Vegas getting married. He had money to burn and he was making a bonfire of it. We stayed in a luxury suite at the Monte Carlo. I was a wreck. Twenty years old on my honeymoon. Then he dropped the bomb about what our marriage was really about—a sexless arrangement, nothing more. I was his beard so that he could pursue his ambitions unburdened by prejudice."

"What did you do then?" Eric asked.

She shook her head. "Nothing. I didn't know what else to do. I just didn't want to be alone again. I was a fucking imbecile and he knew just how to use me. We went back to my mother's house in Dallas. He settled in. A week later…well, you know the rest."

Although she stared into Eric's eyes, she could feel them become intensely still. Neither said a word for what felt like an eternity.

"Megan?" Eric spoke first.

"Yes?"

"Aren't you tired of carrying all this guilt?"

"Guilt?" she asked, confused.

"Yes. Guilt. It's quite a load you're carrying, little one. You feel guilty about your mother's death. You didn't say it but I can see it in your eyes. You feel guilty for falling for Kip. You feel guilty for losing your mother's possessions to the seizure. You feel guilty for not being able to get a divorce, for not being able to keep a job, and for even still being a virgin until you found us. Don't you?"

How could he see into her so deeply? She sighed, pressing her head into his chest. "Yes. I do. All you said is true. I wanted to save my mother. I hated seeing her waste away little by little during all those fucking rounds of chemo. I made her fight even after she was ready to go." She couldn't tamp down her sobs any longer. "You know I was alone when she died. When they wheeled her body out of the room and shut the door behind them, I–I...thought I'd never have a family again. I want to be the kind of woman you guys need. I do. I promise I do."

"You are already that woman, Megan," Scott said.

"No, you don't understand. I don't deserve this. I don't deserve you."

Eric's face darkened, and she felt a shiver shoot through her. His displeasure was terrifying to look at, so she turned her gaze to the floor.

She felt his fingers on her nipples again, tightening even more, pulling her attention back to him and away from her doubts. "You don't think we know what you deserve?" His icy-blue stare reached deep into her, blasting away uncertainties. "We know."

Eric's lips crashed against hers, making her dizzy. One of his hands was on her neck and the other was on the small of her back. He pulled her in tighter into his kiss. She parted her lips, surrendering to his advancing tongue. He deepened their kiss, and she felt her whole body begin to melt into his. A tingle spread from her belly down her thighs.

Without a word, Eric ended their kiss and turned her to face the other Knight in the room.

"We know what you deserve," Scott said. And then he pulled her into his body, pressing her mouth with his. Her head spun, not with doubt this time, but with knowing. They were her knights, her men. Tremors spread through her, heating her body up.

And then the kissing ended just as suddenly as it had begun. Her lips were throbbing as much as her nipples were now.

"She wants more, bro." Scott sent her a wicked wink.

"Not now. Jason is waiting for us. I told him it would only be a minute. We're past that." Eric looked at her. "Unless you don't mind if Jason watches."

She gasped.

He laughed and so did Scott.

"Our Megan is something else, isn't she?" Scott asked.

"That she is." Eric punched the button again, and the big doors unlocked and opened.

Megan knew her cheeks had to be bright red, but she hoped Jason wouldn't notice.

The sheriff walked in and smiled. Damn, he knew what had happened. Were all the men in Destiny in cahoots?

"Give it to us, Jason. What do you have for us?"

"Sorry, guys. Still no sign of Vicky. Her condo looks like she left in a hurry."

"Fuck. Is that all?"

"No. I actually have a favor to ask." Jason opened the file on her desk. The police photos inside were of a bloody murder with two bodies. "These are the two tattooed thugs we got last week who were going to testify against Sergei's father, Niklaus."

"Protective custody isn't what it used to be." Scott spread out the photos, and Megan thought she might actually get sick.

"You're telling me," Jason said. "That's why I'm here. I smell a rat and a cyber one at that."

She couldn't seem to make herself look away from the images of the dead men. Her stomach lurched again, but she was able to breathe through it.

"What makes you think that?" Eric asked.

The sheriff shrugged. "Just a hunch, but I've learned a long time ago to trust my hunches."

"So much blood." The memory of the day her mother's nose started bleeding washed over her like a sickening wave. It happened during her last chemo infusion and the doctors and nurses were trying to get the bleeding to stop but it wouldn't. It never did.

Eric moved in front of her, blocking the images from her view. "This is too much for you, isn't it?"

She nodded.

"That's what I thought," he said. "Jason, we'll take this to the conference room."

"Can't, bro." Scott shook his head. "Techs have it for a video meeting with New Delhi."

"Then let's use room five."

Scott typed something on his iPad. "It's free until two."

"We don't need it for more than fifteen minutes, right, Jason?" Eric asked.

"Sure." The sheriff looked at her. "I'm sorry, Megan. I've been in law enforcement so long I forget about how these kinds of pictures can impact people." He tapped the now-closed file on her desk before picking it up.

"Don't worry about it. I think I'm just hungry."

"We'll be right back, baby." Scott said. "You sure you're okay now?"

"I'm fine," she fibbed. "Go. Hurry back. I would love a burger."

"That's my girl."

"*Our* girl," Eric corrected.

"Agreed," Scott said.

The three of them left her alone in the PFS. She heard the lock engage.

She walked over to the kitchenette. A little water would settle her nerves down. She got a bottle and took a sip.

Even several minutes after the guys had left, her head was still spinning. There were four very good reasons for that. One, she was hungry. Two, she'd confessed her deepest feelings to her guys. Three, they'd kissed her into submission. And finally, those police photos had horrified her. It would take a while for her thoughts to settle down. She was a complete wreck at the moment.

"Megan?" she heard Erica's voice come through from the hidden speaker.

"Coming." She walked over to the release button on the wall.

She wasn't supposed to open the door to anyone, not even Erica. She shook her head. That was the guys' rules. They were overprotective of her in every way. What harm could happen with their secretary, especially on this top floor which only a few trusted people could get to? Besides, she could use the company after seeing those horrible photos Jason had brought.

As Megan hit the button, she heard Erica scream, "Don't open the door. He's got a gun."

Listening to the sound of the lock disengaging, the last five years came crashing into her mind. Was Kip on the other side of that door? She pressed on the button again and again, praying her mistake could be taken back. But it couldn't. She should've followed Eric and Scott's instructions to the letter. *Too late for that now.* As the door swung open, she braced herself to face the monster on the other side.

Chapter Fifteen

Megan's entire body tensed. *Please, God, let this be a horrible nightmare.*

The heavy door to the office swung wide open.

Not Kip.

A man she recalled seeing in the courtroom her first day in Destiny held a gun to Erica's head. He was balding and heavy. He wore a crumpled suit, white shirt, and striped tie. Without the gun and in another place, the man would appear harmless. But he *was* holding a gun and he *was* here.

As always, the automatic doors closed, followed by the sound of the locking mechanism.

Trapped with a monster.

"Megan, I'm so sorry." Erica's panicky eyes multiplied her own dread.

"Shut the fuck up, Erica." The horror turned his attention away from the Knight's secretary and glared at Megan with his dead-looking eyes. "Have a seat, Mrs. Lunceford," he ordered.

She did as he said, praying for Eric and Scott's quick return. "You already know me. Who are you?"

"My name is Felix Averson." The madman pushed Erica away from him. His tone changed to a sickly sweet timbre. "Be a doll and go sit on the floor by Megan's feet."

"Felix, why are you doing this?" Erica asked.

Erica knew him. Did he work at TBK? He must. How else did he get up to the top floor? "Are you selling our stuff to the Chinese, too?"

The bastard hit Erica hard in the face with his fist. She stumbled back, her hands coming up to the injury.

"Tsk-tsk. That's going to leave you with quite the shiner, sweetheart." Felix was right. The swelling in Erica's left eye was already present. Better a black eye than a bullet in the chest. "Now, get on the floor like I told you to." He shoved her down, and Erica landed at Megan's feet.

Erica scrambled next to her and they wrapped their arms around each other in a silent attempt at comfort.

The more time Megan could squeeze out of him the more chance for her protectors to return. "You know each other?"

"Shut the fuck up, bitch." Felix glared at her and then turned back to Erica. "I told you in the other room to keep your mouth shut and you didn't listen. See what that gets you, honey?"

"Take whatever you want, mister." Megan's fear wouldn't back down but she was able to shove it away some. Not ideal but better than it taking over her whole being, paralyzing her completely. She should've been smarter and not hit the button. But she hadn't been. Whatever the excuse—fatigue, hunger, Jason's photos—she'd blown it. There was no way she could take that back now. All she could do was move forward and try not to fuck up again. She'd survived so much already and finally found true love. No way was she going down without a fight. She wasn't the twenty-year-old girl who Kip had deceived any longer, but she still could bleed. *I've got to be smart.*

"You think I'm interested in money, bitch?" The monster walked over to Eric's desk and took a seat. He placed the gun on the desktop, which didn't make her feel better, but she was glad the deadly weapon was there instead of in his hand. "This is about justice."

"What kind of justice are you looking for?" Megan asked, unsure if she should remain quiet or keep him talking. Since she didn't know, she chose the latter. If Felix could think of Erica and her as something more than a target and more like flesh-and-blood people, he might not pull the trigger. She hoped somewhere in Felix was a shred of humanity, unlike Kip, who had no heart.

"Stupid bitch." He pulled out some wires and a small device, connecting it to Eric's computer. Then he typed on Eric's keyboard. "I know where you live, Megan. I was even in your house."

"You're the one who used my Internet access to get into TBK through the back door."

"Right." He glared at the screen.

"Why me?"

"Kip sent me."

Kip? She'd believed all along Kip was pulling the strings in this mess. "Where is he, Felix?"

"In prison, but don't you already know that? Right. You don't know where he is." He turned to her and gave her a twisted grin. "I do."

She'd been trying to find Kip for five years to close a chapter of her life she wanted over. Divorce. That was what she'd always wanted. Surviving this was slim, but she was going to try. *Stall.* "If I'm going to die I, deserve to know Kip's whereabouts. Tell me, please. Where is my husband?" Of course she knew. Her guys had told her. But Felix didn't know that.

"Not a chance, bitch." Felix turned back to the monitor. "Just like my baby said it would be. The password is their parents' death date. You Knights are so predictable."

My baby? Did he mean Kip? Of course he did. "You and Kip are lovers. Is that why you're here?"

"It's part of the reason."

Megan hoped to reach the man somehow. "Felix, you know that our marriage was only for show. I know Kip's secret."

"Shut. The. Fuck. Up. You don't know his secrets at all. I do. Why do you think he reached out to me after his arrest five years ago and not you? He loves me and I love him." The monster typed a few more things into Eric's computer.

She recalled Eric and Scott telling her about their tracking code. Could the other reason Felix was here be to cover his tracks and free Kip and him from the trap her guys had set?

"I'm sure Kip loves you, Felix. He never loved me. I know that." *Keep him talking.*

Felix nodded but never turned away from the computer. "You know Kip is a genius."

"I know." *A psychopathic genius.* "You're in contact with him still?"

"No prison can keep him locked up for long. We have a guy on the inside where he is now. Second in command of the entire place. He's being compensated quite well."

"Impressive. You and Kip must make quite the team."

"Stop your yammering, Mrs. Lunceford, or I swear I'll put a bullet in your head right now. I'll use Erica to be my shield and exit ticket if the two idiot Knight brothers show up. Not the best choice but one I still have. Which will it be?"

She didn't answer, knowing he was on the edge of pulling the trigger.

"Good choice, bitch. Maybe that's how you got your claws into Eric and Scott so fast. God, I couldn't believe it when I saw you talking with them through the window of that burger dive. You're one slick operator, Megan Lunceford. Hell, even Kip can't stop talking about you. It makes me sick. When I relayed what I'd seen the day of your hearing, he knew you would be fucking the billionaire boys in no time at all. I can't understand why Kip is so fascinated with you. He'll be pissed at me for a few days for killing you."

The delusional man had been played by Kip just like her. As terrified as she was at what Felix meant to do to her, she also felt pity for him.

Kip's puppet continued, "I think he wants to kill you himself one day. I can't wait any longer. You have to go. He'll forgive me. He always does." Felix hit another key on the computer. "There you are.

TBK is about to go bye-bye."

And then they all heard the lock disengage.

The demented man grabbed his gun. "Be smart, bitches. You might live a little longer." Then he sent them a murderous stare. Megan knew what he meant to do. But she couldn't let that happen. Not to Eric and Scott. They'd done so much for her. As the door swung open, she screamed, hoping to warn them.

Gretchen rushed in, carrying a couple of bags. "Everything okay here?"

"Who the fuck are you?" Felix asked.

"What in the hell are you doing, Mr. Averson? Don't you remember me? We've met several times over the years that you've been with TBK." Gretchen kept walking forward, dropping the bags. The woman was fearless but also foolish.

"Now I remember you. You're the Knights' stupid servant." Felix pointed the gun at Gretchen. If she didn't stop, he would certainly shoot her.

Megan couldn't let that happen to Gretchen.

It would be like losing her mother all over again.

No.

She had to save her.

As Felix aimed the gun at the center of Gretchen's chest, Megan stood and rushed to her, pushing Gretchen, hopefully out of the line of fire.

Megan heard a gunshot as she and Gretchen fell to the floor together with a loud thump.

Out of the corner of her eye, she saw Eric and Scott—pistols drawn.

More gunshots.

Felix fell to the floor, blood spraying in every direction.

And then silence.

Chapter Sixteen

"You're staying put and that's final. Doctor's orders." Megan sat on the side of Gretchen's bed. Eric and Scott, faces full of relief, stood on the other side of the bed.

"For a flesh wound. Ridiculous." The Knights' all-knowing and loving maid—though she was more like a grandmother to them and now also to Megan—stuck out her tongue. Felix's bullet had grazed Gretchen in her right calf. A few stitches and some rest and the dear lady would be back to normal, at least Gretchen's version of normal.

"Don't push me, Mrs. Hollingsworth." Megan gave her a wink. "You saw what I'm capable of back at TBK. I'm no pushover."

"Indeed, child." Gretchen's eyes brimmed with tears. "When I saw Averson with a gun and you and Erica on the floor, I felt my heart stop in my chest."

"It didn't look like that to me. You were so gutsy."

Gretchen shook her head. "I was terrified, but I couldn't let that madman hurt you two innocent girls. I've lived a very long life. When death comes, I'll be ready."

Scott snorted. "That doesn't mean you have to run headfirst into the grave."

"You ratted me out to my boys, didn't you?" Gretchen asked her with a grin.

Megan smiled. "Told them and the sheriff every minute detail."

Gretchen knew what she was doing, walking straight for the son of a bitch. God, the woman had guts. Too many, in Megan's opinion. Gretchen just might've done it, but at point-blank range the woman would've walked away with much more than a flesh wound.

Everyone, including Gretchen, believed Megan had saved her life. She wasn't so sure, but she was certainly glad that Gretchen was still alive.

"I guess I'll have to fix them English breakfasts every day for a while before they are willing again to let me out of the mansion." Gretchen giggled.

"Not until Doc Ryder releases you, young lady," Eric said in a commanding yet cheerful tone.

"He's barely out of medical school. I know my body, boys. I can run circles around you right now."

"Keep it up and we'll call Doc Ryder back," Scott said. "You can deal with him yourself. But we will be looking forward to those meals once he does give you his seal of approval."

"See, Megan. If you want to win my boys over, always aim for their stomachs." Gretchen held up both her hands in a sign of surrender. "Fine. I'll do as you say, but there's going to be hell to pay if this house isn't kept to my standards, young people."

"Two days is all he asked from you. I think we can keep The Knight Mansion running for forty-eight hours, Gretchen." Scott leaned down and kissed her on the forehead.

"It's not as easy as you might think, lad."

Eric's eyes sparkled brightly. "We won't do half, hell, a quarter of the kind of job you do for us."

"Right about that," Gretchen said.

He leaned down and kissed her on the cheek.

The dear woman sighed. "My sweet boys. Do your best. I'll fix whatever you miss when I get up. And don't you make my precious girl here lift a finger."

"I bet I know more about a vacuum cleaner than either of them do," Megan said.

"You might indeed." Gretchen took the cup of tea Megan had brought her and raised her pinkie as she took a sip. "For now, I suppose I'm a woman of leisure."

"How does it feel?" Megan asked.

"It sucks."

They all burst into laughter, which felt great.

"Ethel is coming over in a little bit to sit with you," Megan told her.

Gretchen's eyes widened. "You've called in the Irish?"

"She's not Irish, and you know it," Scott said.

"She's married to two of them. That makes her Irish in my book." Gretchen smiled. "Why is she coming over anyway?"

"We're taking Megan out tonight." Eric squeezed her hand.

Gretchen grabbed her other hand and squeezed. "Thank you, dear. I don't know what would've happened if you hadn't been so courageous."

"We both were brave, Gretchen."

"Not true." The sweet woman's normally strong voice shook. "This old fool might've gotten us all killed if not for you."

Megan squeezed Gretchen's hands back. "Let's just leave it that we both were foolish and courageous. That's why we're still here."

"How is Erica Coleman doing?" Gretchen asked.

Eric answered, "The black eye will heal, but Sawyer and Reed tell me she's suffering from a big case of guilt. That's going to take longer to get over."

"She's got no reason to be guilty." Megan hated that Erica felt that way. She knew what a heavy load that kind of baggage could be. "Erica tried to save me by screaming. She's the real hero. I pushed the damn button."

"Baby, we've already gone over that. You did nothing wrong." The tenderness in Scott's eyes couldn't be missed.

Eric added, "We shouldn't have left you after seeing those murder scene photos. You were upset."

"I was but I wish I'd been smarter."

"And if you hadn't hit that button, Erica and Gretchen might've been shot by the bastard." Eric's voice softened. "Don't forget,

Megan, Felix had already killed Vicky long before he arrived in Destiny."

Megan closed her eyes tight.

Both Scott and Eric had taken the loss of their longtime employee hard. After the events at TBK, Dallas law enforcement entered Averson's home and found Vicky's body. He'd shot the poor woman just to get her TBK badge to use and to keep suspicion off of him.

Eric reached over Gretchen's bed and touched Megan on the cheek. "Don't blame yourself, little one."

Scott folded his arms over his chest. "The only motherfuckers any of us should be blaming are Felix Averson and Kip Lunceford. Felix is dead and I plan on dealing with Kip myself."

Megan's jaw dropped. "What do you mean by that?" Eric and Scott had known Kip's location. Scott had actually gone and seen him in the Georgia prison. She wasn't angry with them for withholding those details from her, knowing it was their way of trying to keep her out of harm's way. She just didn't want that to happen again. They'd sworn it wouldn't. "Please don't keep things from me, guys. You promised."

"We won't, baby," Scott said. "That's why I'm telling you now. Tonight, we're going to have our date and forget all about the shit that went down at TBK. I'm going to deliver your divorce papers to the asshole tomorrow."

"Shouldn't I go with you to see Kip?" Megan asked.

"Absolutely not," Eric stated firmly. "I don't want you coming within a hundred miles of that psychopath."

"He's contained now, isn't he?" she asked, feeling a sliver of worry spring up inside her.

"Yes, the feds have cut off his way to the outside, thanks to the information you gave them that Felix had told you. They arrested the second-in-command at the prison and beefed up their security around Kip. That still doesn't mean he wouldn't try to get into your head if you were face-to-face with him." Scott definitely meant to keep her safe in both body and mind.

Eric, too. "You're strong and capable, but neither of us want you to be put in that situation again. Understand?"

"Hush, you two." Gretchen's wise eyes were filled with compassion for Megan. "I agree with my boys, dear. Do you really think you need to see this monster for some kind of chance at closure? Hasn't that already occurred for you?"

Megan looked over at Eric and Scott, the men who had turned her life around in so many ways. She'd never felt safe or secure, always listening for the next shoe to drop, watching for the next disaster to appear, and tasting the bitter dregs of her life after Kip.

After Kip.

God, those words meant something far different than before she'd come to Destiny. For five years he was like a dark cloud she could not get out from under. Her life had been ruined *after Kip* had come into it. She lost everything *after Kip's* arrest. Eric and Scott had brought light into her dismal, gray existence. The thick fog Kip had left her had been blown away by them, her cowboys, her protectors, her guys.

After Kip.

It meant he was in the past, a distant memory. Together, she and her loving billionaires had defeated him. Her future had never looked brighter—her future with Eric and Scott by her side.

"Yes, Gretchen. I've had all the closure I need."

Tonight, her men were taking her to Phase Four.

Chapter Seventeen

Megan clasped her hands together to try to keep them from shaking. Eric and Scott, on either side of her, walked her into Phase Four, the BDSM club on West Street not far from Steele Road.

A shiver ran down her spine as they stepped up to the counter of the reception room.

The woman behind the desk was in a leather halter top and Daisy Dukes. The guy behind her was nearly seven foot tall and muscled from head to toe. He wore combat boots, tattered jeans, and a leather vest. His arms were covered in tats and both his ears were pierced and had emeralds in them.

"Here you go, Trixie." Eric handed the lady the papers Megan had already read and signed earlier. "Room three."

Scott waved at the guy by the door. "Hey, Sarge."

The bouncer nodded slightly. She pitied any fool who would try to get past Sarge without the proper invitation.

Trixie handed Eric a key. "Have fun." She gave Megan a wink and then giggled. "I love first timers, don't you, Sarge?"

Again, a single nod came from the man, making her wonder what went on inside his head. Something dark and dangerous most likely.

As her guys walked her into Phase Four's main area, she began to tremble, feeling anxious and expectant.

"Slow night," Scott said.

It didn't look slow to her. The place was bustling with bodies. Phase Four was much bigger than she'd imagined it would be. Most were mingling around the three stages, which were all set to the left side of the massive space. To the right was a dance floor with a bar, which she'd already been told served water or juices only—no beer, wine, or liquor.

On two of the stages *scenes* were being performed.

She looked back and forth at her escorts. God, they were handsome. They obviously could've had their pick here from the stares and smiles coming their direction from many of the women in the place. She was glad Eric and Scott had chosen her outfit, though Eric had been the primary lead on that. She didn't feel so out of place in the leather boots, miniskirt, and white cotton top, which was more snug than she was used to wearing but clearly on the conservative side for Phase Four by what she was seeing.

Her heart hammered in her chest as she saw a woman on the center stage being spanked with the scariest looking paddle she'd ever seen, not that she'd seen many.

She turned her head away, back to the part of Phase Four that looked more like a nightclub than a sex club. The dance floor was bustling with club members. She loved to dance, but had never danced as erotically as the majority of the crowd tonight was. Lasers filled the space and hip-hop music thumped bass notes on her skin.

"What do you think about our club?" Scott's voice rolled out of his mouth like a growl from a predator.

"It's a little overwhelming, Sir." Megan answered as she'd been instructed to back at the mansion. They'd already assumed their roles.

She felt her eyes widen when she spotted the man on the far stage thrashing a woman who was on a thing that looked like a giant *X*, which she knew from her books must've been a St. Andrew's Cross. He was standing about ten feet from her with a whip. Its crack in the air made Megan jump and her heart skip a beat.

Eric pointed across the room. "That's our friend Josh. He's also our pilot. He's one of the club's resident Doms. I don't know who the sub is. Do you, Scott?"

"It looks like Baby to me."

Eric nodded. "Yes, it is Baby."

Baby? Was that her real name? Surely not.

The crack of the whip and Baby's moans were like music. Josh was the conductor, making the symphony. But it was more than that. The little welts he was painting on her flesh were so beautiful. Megan could imagine herself up there with Eric and Scott, feeling the bite of their whips. She squeezed her thighs together, trying to quell the urgency she was feeling in her pussy.

Her nerves were getting the best of her. She'd actually been the one to request this outing. Had that been a mistake? Eric and Scott had jumped on the idea. Now that Felix was dead and Kip couldn't bother them any longer, they might be able to have some fun together. How long had it been since they'd had sex? Her first. Their...? Millionth, probably. That didn't bother her any longer. They'd helped her see that she could trust herself, and thereby, she could trust them.

She liked the Dom attire Eric and Scott were wearing. Leather pants, combat boots, black T-shirts, and black Stetsons. They were her two black knights and she was their princess.

Eric touched her thigh. "Ready, little one?"

Her mouth dropped. "To go up on one of those stages, Sir?"

He grinned. "You're definitely not ready for that one. No. Are you ready to go see the room we had set up for you?"

She tried to answer, but it came out more like a choke. Neither Eric nor Scott looked away. "How, Sir? How did you set up a room for me? We've been together all day."

"She's going to be a handful, Eric."

"Four handfuls, Scott."

Trying to calm herself, she took a deep breath. "Yes, Sir. I'm ready."

Eric cupped her chin and fixed his eyes on her. His stare only made her even more jittery and hot. "Better, little one. Much better. You can ask questions all you want, but you must answer our questions first. Understand?"

"Yes, Sir."

"Color?"

"Green."

"Let's go."

She walked between them through the crowd, thinking about how it had felt to have Scott's cock inside her body. Was tonight when she would get to know what Eric's cock felt like inside her pussy? A whiff of their masculine scent made it into her nose. Musk and leather. Their manly scents sent a tingle into her belly.

They came to a door at the end of a long hallway. Eric pulled out the key and unlocked it.

"Inside, sub." His intensity was like unyielding metal.

"Yes, Sir." She was already shaking and they'd only held her hand. God, she wanted them, needed them, craved them with every shaky breath that was causing her breasts to heave.

She walked in and Eric and Scott followed behind.

"I'm a little nervous, Sirs," she confessed, looking around the room which reminded her a lot of the playroom back at the mansion. There were more sex toys here, but only by a fraction. The bench in the middle of the space looked more versatile with all its hinges and rods. Still, it looked to be set up tonight for spanking to her. *For me.*

"Being nervous can be a good thing, little one." He leaned in and pressed his thick lips to hers. Her toes curled as his tongue swept into her mouth. She could feel the heat growing between her thighs.

"Lock and load time." Scott's tone seemed heavy with possessiveness and hunger.

"That it is, brother. That it is."

They stripped her of her clothes slowly, meticulously, scanning every inch of newly exposed skin. Her insides began to boil under their intense scrutiny. Their rough fingertips skated over her body, making her dizzy and needy.

Her pussy dampened as they dotted kisses on her body where their fingers had just been. Eric and Scott knew how to rev her engine up.

"Have you sucked a cock before, little one?"

She shook her head.

"You will tonight."

"Yes, Sir."

"Color?" Scott asked.

"Green, Sir."

Scott came behind her and Eric in front.

Eric's carnal stare caused her head to spin. "On your knees, sub."

"Yes, Sir." She lowered herself down with their help, their hands on her shoulders and arms.

"That's perfect," Eric said. "Hands behind your back and drop your gaze."

She obeyed.

"Fuck, that's a pretty picture." Scott's words were deep, laden with what sounded to her as limitless lust.

Eric's deep voice rumbled, "Time for me to fill up that sweet mouth with my thick cock."

With her eyes down, she couldn't see but heard Eric unbutton his pants. Then she saw them fall to his feet in a leathery black pile. She felt his fingers on her chin, forcing her to tilt her head up.

She looked at Eric, standing in front of her with his monstrous cock in his other hand. Her cheeks burned and she moved her eyes up to his.

He shook his head. "Not my eyes, sub. My cock. Look at it. Tell me what you see."

"Yes, Sir." She scanned his beautiful dick, taking it all in. "It's thick."

"Go on."

"Long. Nine inches."

"Nine and a half. Very good. And?"

"Your cockhead looks purplish."

He moved his fingers from her chin to her cheek. Scott was stroking her hair from behind. The whole thing was making her wet.

"Time for a sample. Put the tip of your finger on the crown of my cock. That's it. Feel that?"

Her fingers touched a drop of warm liquid. "Yes, Sir."

"That's my pre-cum. That tells you I'm hot for you, little one. God, I'm fucking on fire for you." She'd never heard Eric so impassioned before, and she liked it. "Taste it."

"Yes, Sir." She brought her fingertip up to her mouth.

She stuck out her tongue and licked.

He tasted salty and spicy, and it sent a new bout of shivers through her body and down into her pussy. Drinking on his lust, she couldn't get over the fact that this was really happening. He wanted her. Scott wanted her. And God, how she wanted them. She wanted to touch them, to caress their muscles, enjoy the feel of their bronzed bodies on her fingers. These were her saviors, her protectors, her lovers. They'd done so much for her, and more than anything, she wanted to be the woman that would please them the way they deserved to be pleased.

Eric stepped forward, placing his big feet on the outside of her thighs. "I don't want you to open your mouth yet, understand?"

She nodded, actually feeling the heat coming off his body on her skin.

"I want you to get comfortable with my cock. Kiss it."

She kissed the middle of his shaft.

"Unclasp your hands, little one, and touch my dick. Get to know how it feels."

Scott rubbed her shoulders, which felt wonderful, while she followed all of Eric's instructions to the letter. She held him in her hand, and could actually feel his pulse in his cock. She leaned in, inhaling his scent of musk and spice.

"Gently cup my balls, sub."

"Yes, Sir." They felt heavy in her hands.

"You want to taste me, little one?"

She nodded, as hot trembles raced through her belly and down her thighs.

"I want that, too."

She kissed his balls, which were tight against his body.

Eric blew out a hot, lusty breath.

"Hard for you to keep your own control with our pet, isn't it?" Scott asked. "I've never seen you so unhinged before, bro."

"And I know you're loving it, aren't you? Don't worry about me. She needs us more than ever to keep our heads."

"Agreed."

Eric moved his hands to her hair. His fingers threaded through her locks, raising her temperature another degree. He smiled down, his face kind, his deep blue eyes devastating her. "You've never done this before, so I want you to listen hard to what I'm about to say, okay?"

"Yes, Sir."

His left hand moved to her neck. "There's a gag reflex inside this pretty little throat. It's natural as can be. I don't want you trying to prove anything by pushing yourself too far. Tonight, I want you to lick the head of my cock and then put it in your mouth. That's all until I tell you otherwise, little one."

Tears pricked at the back of her eyes. God, whenever he called her that, everything inside her came alive. The tenderness she'd sensed in him early on was now out in the open and pointed right at the center of her heart. He and Scott had captured all of her being. She was theirs. No doubt about it.

It was as if every thought that entered her mind, they could hear, every emotion that sprung inside her, they could sense. But it didn't end with them knowing her inner workings better than she knew them herself. These brothers became whatever she needed them to be— tough and demanding sometimes, gentle and indulgent at other times.

She kissed Eric's cockhead, relishing the fresh drop of pre-cum on her lips. She licked the saltiness of Eric's essence and looked up as his eyes narrowed into a hungry stare.

"Open your mouth and take in the crown. Don't suck on it yet." His words, though tender, held a tinge of risk and passion. He was on the edge of his control, and that made her both jittery and ecstatic.

She opened her mouth wide and moved her lips to the head of his cock.

He groaned a little, and she felt for a brief second his hand press lightly on the back of her head. "Damn, I feel like a teenage boy with her."

Scott laughed. "See how you're getting to him, sweetheart? Mr. Control is having trouble. I love it. You better not shoot your load down her pretty little virgin throat."

"Shut the fuck up. I'm trying to concentrate here." Eric's breathing was heavy.

Megan loved the impact she was having on him. Keeping his crown in her mouth, she rolled her tongue over his cock slit and was rewarded with another drop of deliciousness.

"Holy hell, Megan," Eric blew out. "Damn, that feels good. Okay, you can suck me now."

She sucked hard, hollowing out her cheeks, continuing to swirl her tongue around his cockhead. Scott shifted to the floor behind her, and then his hands came around and cupped her breasts. His lips kissed the back of her neck, causing her to moan into Eric's cock inside her mouth.

"Enough," Eric groaned. "I know my fucking limits and I'm already there. One more lick, little one, and then we move on to the next phase of tonight's activities."

"Shouldn't our sub try to swallow a cock fully at least once?" Scott said, his teasing, brotherly tone not lost on her.

"Yes. She should. It's important. Give me a second." Eric buried his hand in her hair again. "Okay, little one. I want you to relax your throat. Think about how you would open your mouth and say 'ah' at the dentist. It's the same thing without the sound. If you understand me, squeeze my cock with your right hand.

Keeping his cockhead in her mouth, she squeezed his shaft as he'd told her to do.

"Okay, ready?"

She squeezed him again.

He thrust lightly in and out of her mouth, sending his cock a fraction of an inch deeper down her throat.

"Look at that pretty little cocksucker go." Scott gently massaged her breast. "How's she doing?"

Eric groaned. "She's killing me. Fuck. Feels good." His self-control was something to behold. He was on the edge of release but held himself steady. She could feel the pulse of his cock thudding harder and harder against her lips. She wanted to take more of him, more inches. She didn't even have three inches of Eric down her throat yet.

Ahhh. Her throat was tightening and panic crawled at the edge of her consciousness.

"Enough." Eric pulled out of her mouth, once again clearly sensing her emotions before they got the better of her. He brushed the hair out of her eyes. "You did great, little one. Really good."

"Her first time and she nearly sent you to the moon," Scott said, continuing torturing her breasts with his fingertips. "Can you imagine how good she's going to be in a few weeks?"

"God no. Imagine how she'll be in a couple of months. If we aren't very careful, she'll be the one in control, not us."

His praise unraveled her and ignited every feminine part of her.

She felt a slight tug on her hair from behind.

"That won't be happening," Scott said. "In our bedroom, in our playroom, and here at Phase Four, she's our sub. We are in control. Always."

"Agreed." Eric stepped out of his pants, which had been down around his ankles. His monstrous cock was straight up and glistening with her saliva. Then he removed the rest of his clothes in a flash. His ripped, muscled body was right in front of her. She wanted to reach out and touch him, but she didn't, remembering the protocols they'd already taught her. "I'm ready to take her virginity."

She wasn't sure what he meant by that. Hadn't Scott already done that the other night? Of course he had.

Scott laughed, his hands moving up and down her arms. "Our sub is confused."

Eric smiled. "I asked you the other night if you had ever had anal sex. You told us you'd never had any kind of sex before. Well, tonight, I will be the first man to claim your pretty ass, little one."

Her anxiety shot up.

She felt Scott's lips on her ears. "Trust us, Megan. What color are you?"

They'd proven time and again they deserved her trust. She did trust them.

Though the tiniest of anxiety remained about what they were about to do to her, she said, "Green, Sirs. I'm green."

They lifted her up together and placed her facedown on the bench that was bent in the middle. Her heartbeats raced in her chest as she felt Eric's hands cup her ass.

Out of the corner of her eye, she saw Scott strip out of his clothes.

"Don't move, little one."

She felt Eric apply lubricant to her anus with his thick fingers. Scott went to the table with all the sex toys.

Scott came back with a purple dildo. "This will do fine."

Did they mean to put that thing in her ass? It was too big, though it was a little smaller than either of their cocks were.

"Scott, cuff her wrists but leave her ankles alone." Eric's fingers circled the tight ring of her ass, continuing to apply more lube.

She trembled, worrying about what was about to come. Could she take a dildo into her ass and survive? What if she hated it? What then? Was that the kind of woman they needed? The old doubts bubbled to the surface, drowning her in worry.

"Agreed." Scott placed the handcuffs on her wrists and then attached them to the rings on the bench. "I think a few spanks will get our baby out of her head.

"Absolutely on board with that idea." Eric actually sounded eager. "Little one, do you trust us?"

"Yes, Sir." Her clit began to throb but all she could think about was how in the world she would be able to take Eric's monstrous cock in her ass.

She felt the sting of the first whack on her cheeks. It hadn't come from an open hand but from something harder.

As if on cue, Scott placed the offending paddle in front of her face. It looked brutal and so very dangerous. "See this? Take a good look at this, sub."

It was a wicked black and was terrifyingly big.

"This is going to help us get you out of your head so you can enjoy some real pleasure."

Another whack landed on her ass, delivering a hot bite. Another fell on a different part of her bottom, and she started to shiver. Another came. And another. *Whack. Whack.* Her ass began to burn and she chewed on her lower lip, trying to hold back the tears that were pricking her eyes.

Eric patted her ass, reminding her what he intended to do. God, she wanted to be all he wanted her to be, but she just wasn't sure it was possible, despite what her treasured books told her.

"Still in her head," Scott said.

"I know." Eric tugged on her hair. "Color?"

"Green, Sirs," she panted out.

Rapid-fire blows from Eric's open hand rained down on her ass. *Spank. Spank. Spank.*

Her doubts scampered away, leaving only the hot sensations emanating from the devastating stings on her ass into her belly and down her thighs.

She was so hot, on fire even, her ache expanding and stretching. She closed her eyes and the tears fell. Manly lips touched her mouth and she opened her eyes and saw Scott's brown beauties staring back at her.

Eric sent his fingers into her ass and she gasped. She could feel her pussy dampening, spilling her cream on the bench. Her clit throbbed and she writhed under Eric's finger assault into her ass. He stretched her with more thrusts, adding another finger to his work.

Her breathing became labored, every nerve ending in her body firing. She wanted to prove she could do this, wanted to prove to her men she was the woman they wanted her to be.

"What color, little one?"

"Green, Sirs."

Eric stroked her ass in a way that clearly let her know that he was to be trusted, that he knew what he was doing, and that he intended on doing it. His gentle, caressing fingertips were reassurances that he wouldn't push her beyond her limits, beyond her ability to tolerate.

She would take him. He deserved her other virginity. He would take it and she would willingly surrender it to him.

"Take in a deep breath for us, baby," Scott commanded.

She did, filling her lungs to the maximum of their capacity.

"Blow it out all at once."

Again, she obeyed, letting the air rush out in a single giant exhalation.

"Big, calming breath. Good. Very good. Now, blow it out again."

As the last ounce of air passed her lips, she felt the toy get shoved into her ass. The collision of plastic toy to virgin flesh shocked her into a dizzy state. She was being spread apart, stretched wide. Again, manly lips pressed on her feminine mouth. She kept her eyes tight, fighting to hold on. The kiss helped. So did the hands on her body. When she felt a thumb press on her clit, she screamed into Scott's unrelenting mouth.

The pain had morphed into need inside her body. She wanted Eric, wanted him to take her where she'd never been taken.

"She's ready, bro."

"That's enough plug for you tonight." Eric kissed the side of her face. "Time to fill up this sweet virgin ass with my dick, little one."

The toy and handcuffs were removed, leaving her aching for more. She needed to feel him inside her, be possessed in that way. She felt Eric's naked body cover her back, his weight restraining her more than the cuffs ever had. When she felt the head of his cock on her anus, she wiggled her hips for him to enter, her need so intense, so consuming.

"You're going to be trouble, little one. I can see that clearly." His voice had an edge of threat that made her tremble. "Who is in charge here? You or your Doms—Scott and me?"

A little grin spread across her face. *My Doms.* "You are, Sirs. You are in charge."

"Excellent. Now, let me do my Dom job and take your virgin ass the way it was meant to be taken." He kissed the back of her head, and she moaned into Scott's lips.

Eric thrust his cock into her ass, and her entire body seemed to vibrate. She was stretched and so very full. As the pain backed down, she was racked with zipping tingles that ran up and down her body, one after another and another and another.

Suddenly she was pulled off the bench. Eric's cock remained deeply seated in her ass as his back hit the floor. Scott hovered above her with his thick, monstrous cock in his fist. If Eric was acting as her mattress, then Scott was her blanket. Her lips trembled as Scott slowly, ever so slowly, sent his cock into her weeping pussy. Every hungry stroke forward into her channel ignited more desire and more need than before. Their hard cocks were filling her beyond what she thought possible. She wrapped her legs around Scott's waist and her arms around his neck.

"Squeeze our dicks, little one." Eric growled. "Feel us inside you."

She obeyed, tightening her pussy and her ass around their thickness.

Scott placed one hand on the floor to steady himself and continued his assault. The other one he sent between them until his fingertips were on her clit. His touch multiplied her already crazed suffering.

As their thrusts synced up, her body began to writhe like mad. She was close to the edge of an orgasm. So close.

"Feels so good, Sirs," she panted, unable to remain quiet.

"Yeah it feels good, sub. It feels fucking amazing." Scott's control was tossed aside now and he pounded into her, a man lost to his passions.

"Come for us, little one." Eric's breathing and tone told her he was on the brink of losing his control, too.

Something about this moment, with her men claiming her utterly, with her body buzzing like mad, with the knowledge that this was only the beginning of her life with Eric and Scott, turned up the heat and sent her rocketing past her boundaries to the orgasm she so desperately needed.

It erupted in a sea of sensations zipping through her body like hot electricity, exploding along every path of nerves, every line of tingles, every gasp for air. She never knew a scream could be joyous and so intoxicating until this very moment. She wasn't sure if this room at Phase Four was soundproof or not, but she didn't care who heard her. She had to let it out. Her euphoria was too big to be contained in her body.

"Fuuck. Ahhh." Scott's climax was reflected all over his handsome face. She could feel the pulse of his cock in her pussy, which was convulsing around his shaft again and again.

Then she felt Eric's final thrust into her ass. "Yesss." His word drew out in a steamy hiss as he came inside her ass.

"Oh God!" she screamed, as another fresh round of wild tingles ripped through her flesh. Her womb tightened, released, and then tightened again, over and over.

How long she remained sandwiched between Eric and Scott, she couldn't tell. She was completely spent, barely holding on to consciousness.

Scott hoisted her up off the floor and off of Eric. She leaned into his chest, her legs still wrapped around his waist.

The brothers pulled out towels from a cabinet she'd failed to see when they'd come into the room. There was also a sink. She was completely wrung out, and the tingles continued as they cleaned her entire body and applied soothing lotion to her freshly spanked, stinging bottom. They dressed her together. Scott kissed and caressed her lightly as Eric put on his clothes. Then the brothers traded places, and Eric feathered his lips over her lips, nose, and eyes.

As they walked her out of Phase Four, keeping her eyes open was proving to be a difficult task. The past few days had been so long. She could've died the other day. Gretchen could've died, too. Her men might've been killed. But none of that had happened.

Once outside, Eric lifted her up in his arms. The cloudless night was filled with stars.

They piled into his truck for the two-minute, three-block drive back to their mansion. *Our mansion.* Her exhausted giggle came out more like a pant.

Scott carried her inside and up to *their* room, the one Eric and Scott had given her the first day she'd come to Destiny. The one with the big, comfy bed.

They undressed her and placed her in the center of the mattress. She watched her two billionaires strip out of their clothes.

Scott crawled in beside her on the right. He kissed her. "God, you're beautiful. How did I ever live without you?"

"I don't know," she said, sounding more feminine than ever before.

He kissed her again. "I love you, Megan."

"I love you, too."

Eric got in the bed on her left. She rolled to face him. His gaze captured her eyes entirely. "I love you, little one." He kissed her, sweeping his tongue tenderly into her greedy mouth. "I'll always love you."

"I love you, too."

Slowly, she drifted closer and closer to a slumber that would've never been possible just a week ago. What a whirlwind romance, but she had no doubt what had begun in such a short amount of time would last for the rest of her life.

Scott's laugh pulled her back to consciousness.

"What's so funny?" Eric asked.

"I just thought that if we hadn't sued Megan, we would've never found her. Proof positive that something good can come from lawyers after all. Cam's going to love hearing that."

They all lost themselves in fits of laughter.

Megan was finally home.

Chapter Eighteen

Once again, Scott sat on the bench facing Kip's unique prison cell, but this time he was the one smiling, not the asshole.

Kip sat on the metal bench bolted to the wall in his cage reading Megan's divorce papers.

The security had definitely been beefed up since Scott's last visit. Though it would've been nice to hand the legal forms to Kip himself, Scott followed the new protocols the prison warden had set up for the madman. In truth, he was relieved, knowing Kip would never be able to reach Megan again.

It had taken several hours and tons of paperwork to get the divorce documents to Kip. Scott wasn't sure how that had happened, but suspected anything given to the bastard was handled with great caution. When the armed guard, who was still standing by, had led him here, Kip already had them.

Kip looked up from the pages and frowned. "You seriously think I will sign these without talking to my wife in person?"

"Sign. Don't sign. It doesn't change the fact that a divorce will be granted for Megan."

"Then why even ask for it, Scott? If you don't need my signature, why come here at all?"

"I wanted to tell you myself that you will never see her again. You will never be able to harm her again." Scott leaned forward and tapped on the Plexiglas. "Now that your lover and the prison traitor are out of the picture, I think this box will hold you."

Kip's face darkened with rage and he threw the divorce papers to the floor of his cell. "Fuck you, Knight. Do you think I care a fuck whether Felix or the other guy live or die? I don't. I know what is important. I know what matters. Fuck you and all your Destiny Luddites. The world has changed. People like me have the power. Real power. I will win. Nothing can hold someone like me."

Scott made the same buzzing sound that Kip had given his first visit. "Wrong. You've lost."

"My code is still sleeping inside TBK's systems."

He wasn't about to tell the bastard that he and Eric had already hired two of the best minds to unravel the destructive viruses planted by Felix, Kip's patsy, into the TBK network. It would take months but it would be done.

Kip continued ranting, lost in his lunacy. "You'll see. I will win. I will win. I will win."

Scott stood up, smiled, and said, "Game over."

* * * *

Inside the limo, Megan couldn't believe her contract with Eric and Scott was less than a week from completion. She sat between them in the stretch that was heading to her mother's house. Even though thrilled to see it again, she was apprehensive, too. Eric had seen it when he'd come for the modem, but Scott hadn't.

She'd flown with her guys on the TBK jet to Dallas, along with Norman, who was coming out of retirement and out of the burger shop kitchen to fill the void left by the two dead executives, one good and one bad.

After the meeting at the headquarters with the board, Eric and Scott had been evasive when she'd reminded them her three-month contract was coming to an end. Her two Doms hadn't come right out and asked her to stay past the negotiated time. What would happen after? Both had told her time and again how much they loved her. She couldn't imagine her life without them.

"Here we are," Eric announced as the limo turned the corner onto the street where her mother's house resided.

Her jaw dropped at the change she saw in the tiny place. The Texas sun was low in the sky on this cloudless Sunday night, but the new landscaping around the space created a phenomenal curb appeal.

"When did you do this?" she asked, grabbing both their hands and squeezing as the stretch parked in front of her home. She spotted a couple of neighbors peering out their windows.

Eric kissed her cheek. "You've been busy with the paintball event. We were busy with this."

She sighed, feeling her heart leap in her chest. "And running a billion-dollar company, too."

"That's easy, baby." Scott stroked her hair. "The job we love is making you happy. How are we doing so far?"

"Amazing."

They all got out of the vehicle.

Megan stood outside her mother's home with Eric and Scott on either side of her. The lighting and flowers made it look like a showplace. Even the formerly cracked driveway had been repaired. "I can't believe you've done this for me."

"You like, little one?" Eric asked.

"I love it." She leaned into him. "How did you get this done so fast?"

"Wait, baby," Scott said. "There's more to show you. This is just the gift wrapping."

"There's more?"

"Come and see," Eric said, motioning her forward.

Walking up to the front porch, the leaky overhang was gone. In its place was a covering that offered protection from the changeable weather conditions normal for Texas.

"This looks like the cover of a magazine," she told them, feeling overwhelmed and happy. Three crisp white rocking chairs sat to the right of the front door—one for each of them. "Why did you do this?"

"For you," Scott said. "Besides, we've wanted a permanent residence when we come to meetings in Dallas. Your house is perfect for us."

"More to see, little one," Eric said, opening the door and leading her in.

A single step in and her breath was taken away. "Oh my God."

Several chopped-up rooms of her home had been combined into one big space, creating a great room. *Great. It certainly is.*

The threadbare carpet had been replaced by beautiful hardwood flooring. The walls were painted a soft hue of green. Everything was working. The lights. The ceiling fan. The new flat screen mounted on the wall. Her tiny block of a TV was no more.

The room had a relaxed vibe. Big comfy chairs and a sofa that looked casual yet she was certain cost a fortune. The wall that had divided this room from the kitchen and small dinning area was gone. Open. God, she loved the feel of the space now. Looking into the kitchen, she saw top-of-the-line stainless-steel appliances. No surface had been untouched. In place of the orange laminate was gorgeous granite. The former vinyl floor was now tiled in a lush earth tone.

As the tour continued, she was filled with awe and gratitude. She could've never done or even imagined this. The final stop was her bedroom. It looked like the most inviting place she'd ever seen. A fluffy California king-size bed was in the center of the room. On the bed were two recognizable gift bags in Tiffany blue.

"No more gifts. This is too much already." Happy tears brimmed in her eyes. "Thank you, guys. I don't know what to say."

Eric and Scott smiled, each taking one of the bags and pulling out the item inside each.

Eric held a silver collar and Scott a diamond ring.

Then her cowboys both got down on their knees.

"I hope you say you'll marry me," Scott said.

"And me," Eric chimed in. "Marry us, little one."

"Make us the happiest men in the world, baby," Scott added.

Joyous tears streamed down her cheeks. "Yes, I'll marry you. I've just become the happiest woman in the world."

They scooped her up in their arms, squeezing her between them.

As Eric and Scott lowered her down onto the soft bed, her heart swelled in her chest. She looked up at the ceiling, which was now vaulted. Her mother had dreamed about doing that. It was part of their lottery game—*when we win the lottery we'll...* Then she looked at Eric and Scott and realized she'd done much better than that. She'd won her future, her destiny with her two loving billionaires.

* * * *

Eric watched the paintball gamers running around Destiny, which was completely draped in tarps and plastic for the event. He and Scott stood behind Megan, who was sitting in front of The Red Dragon at the judges' table. Phoebe, Amber, and Amber's sister, Belle, were sitting with her, each typing away on laptops and fielding questions from participants. Megan and the other women were forming a very tight bond. In fact, they were all working on wedding plans together, which was set for October, a week before the O'Learys' big Halloween party.

Megan leaned in and clicked the microphone in front of her. "Two minutes left in this round until the final buzzer, players."

God, he was so proud of Megan. Destiny's Annual Paintball Extravaganza had never been better. She'd doubled the take and reduced the expenditures by half, allowing them to raise over a hundred thousand dollars for Amber Stone's new boys' ranch. With the matching proceeds from the O'Learys, TBK, Jennifer Steele, and the Stone brothers, that brought the total donation up to half a million bucks. Having lost his own parents, Eric was glad the town would be teeming with new orphans soon.

Jason and his brothers, Mitchell and Lucas, stepped up to the table. Odd, since the three rarely spent time together. That was more

Lucas's fault than Mitchell's, though both had been hard on Jason after the breakup with Phoebe. It was good to see them around each other, though none of them seemed thrilled about it. The truth was that this event and Dragon Week were the only times the Wolfe brothers convened. Everyone knew they were Destiny's best volunteers.

A big spot of blue was right in the center of the sheriff's uniform, which made Eric smile.

"I see they got you again, Jason," Scott said.

"Every fucking year. I wish these gamers would read the rules and abide by them."

"Same old Jason. Always in love with your rules." Phoebe stood up, glaring at the sheriff. "Megan, do you mind if I take a break now?"

Megan nodded. "Sure thing. We've got things covered until the next bout."

"I'll be back before that starts. I just need some air." Phoebe turned and walked to the food tent, which was just on the other side of The Red Dragon.

"Goddamn it, Jason." Lucas's ancient loss of the woman of his dreams had fueled a lot of animosity between him and Jason. "I need a break, too, Megan."

"Me, too," Mitchell chimed in. He had buried the axe between him and Jason to a point but still blamed the older brother for the breakup. Sometimes the old wound would fester, like now.

"Sure thing, guys. Go." Megan didn't look up from her laptop. She was so focused, but more than that, she was beautiful and she was his and Scott's.

"Number twenty-eight on the blue team and number thirteen on the red team are out," Jason's deputy, Charlie, yelled from across the street. "Firing in a no-fire zone."

"Got it. Thanks, Charlie," Amber said.

Charlie was reprimanding the two participants. He was going to be missed.

Eric hated to see him go, but understood completely why Charlie wanted to be with his kids. What he never would understand was what had happened to him and his ex, Aimee. Eric hoped they might be able to reconcile their differences, at least for their boys.

Eric looked at Megan, imagining her pregnant with their child. God, he couldn't wait for that day.

"I don't need more shit," Jason snapped, staring at his brothers' backs as they walked away. "I've got too much on my plate already."

"Like what?" Scott asked.

Jason blew out a big hot breath of frustration. "I haven't even finished the state's paperwork on the Stones' big shootout let alone even starting on the mess that happened at your offices. With those two witnesses dead, Niklaus Mitrofanov is being released. The feds don't have enough to hold him."

"Can you guys please be quiet?" Belle snapped, and then suddenly became excited, pointing to one of the gamers. "Amber, there's Juan. Do you see him?"

"Yes. He's doing great, too."

Jason lowered his voice. "I'm looking into why Niklaus's son, Sergei, was on Amber's missing persons report as her husband. I spoke with the officer who filed the report, Officer Nicole Flowers."

"What did you learn?" Eric asked.

"Not much except she's a handful. Against my wishes, she's coming here."

Emmett, Bryant, and Cody Stone walked to the judges' table with Sawyer and Reed Coleman, their ranch hands. Of course, they were much more than that. They were all like brothers to Eric and Scott, having all lost their parents in the same plane crash a couple of weeks after 9/11.

Cody leaned over the table and kissed Amber. "Hey, baby."

She blushed. "Can't you see I'm working, cowboy?"

"Can't you see I'm in love?" he asked.

Jason turned to Sawyer and Reed. "You two might be able to help me with a problem I have heading to town."

"What problem?" Sawyer asked.

Before Jason could answer the game buzzer went off.

Megan clicked on her microphone. "That's the end of the round, players."

The gamers started lining up in front of the table to claim their shots. The two that got everyone's attention instantly moved to the front of the line. When they took off their goggles and masks, there was a uniform gasp from the other players.

Gretchen and Ethel were arguing over who shot who.

Eric smiled, watching Megan take charge like the pro she was. Thank God, he and Scott had decided to sue her. It brought her, the woman he would love for the rest of his life, to Destiny, a place like nowhere else on earth. A place where misfits, castaways, and even two elderly women who enjoyed a good game of paintball were welcome. Destiny was his home. He placed his hands on Megan's shoulders. She turned and smiled. This tiny town in northern Colorado had always been his and Scott's home. Now, it was Megan's too.

Destiny was where they all belonged together, now and forever.

THE END

WWW.CHLOELANG.COM

ABOUT THE AUTHOR

Chloe Lang began devouring romance novels during summers between college semesters as a respite to the rigors of her studies. Soon, her lifelong addiction was born, and to this day, she typically reads three or four books every week.

For years, the very shy Chloe tried her hand at writing romance stories, but shared them with no one. After many months of prodding by an author friend, Sophie Oak, she finally relented and let Sophie read one. As the prodding turned to gentle shoves, Chloe ultimately did submit something to Siren-BookStrand. The thrill of a life happened for her when she got the word that her book would be published.

For all titles by Chloe Lang, please visit
www.bookstrand.com/chloe-lang

Siren Publishing, Inc.
www.SirenPublishing.com

CPSIA information can be obtained at www.ICGtesting.com
Printed in the USA
BVOW04s1012200514

354052BV00022B/691/P